Young Master Darcy

A Lesson in Honour

by
Pamela Aidan

Wytherngate Press
2010

2010 Wytherngate Press

Cover portrait
Master James Hatch by Sir William Beechy

ISBN-13 978-0-9831031-0-3
LCCN: 2010939609

Wytherngate Press website: wytherngatepress.com

The principal text of this book was set in a digitized version of 11.5 point
Baskerville. Title appears in Edwardian Script.

Printed in the United States of America on acid-free paper.

Aidan, Pamela
  Young Master Darcy: A Lesson in Honour/ Pamela Aidan
  120p.; 21 cm.
  Series: Young Master Darcy; 1.
  ISBN-13 978-0-9831031-0-3
  1. Regency–England–Fiction. 2. Regency fiction. I.
Austen, Jane, 1775-1817. Pride and Prejudice. II. Series:
Young Master Darcy : A Lesson in Honour; Book 1.

  813.6   2010939609

TABLE OF CHAPTERS

Chapter 1	5
Chapter 2	20
Chapter 3	36
Chapter 4	47
Chapter 5	60
Chapter 6	76
Chapter 7	95
Chapter 8	107

–&–

For our grandchildren: Madison, Connor, Katherine,
Madelyn, Jackson, and Sophie...

–&–

Chapter 1

The carriage rocked gently now as the driver began to pick his way through the teaming traffic of London. Master Fitzwilliam George Alexander Darcy sat up from his slouched position, an attitude that would have called forth his father's rebuke at such thoughtless indulgence, and pressed his thirteen-year-old face to the cold window. He was in a familiar part of Town, not far from his family's London home, and nothing particularly remarkable presented itself to his gaze. *That was disappointing!* He had been away and on his own for several months. It seemed only right that, as he had changed during that time, so would the rest of the world.

The jangle of harness and the shouts of post riders penetrated the carriage. Curious, Darcy sat up even straighter and peered forward as far as the closed window would allow. *Not enough!* Impulsively, he pulled down the window and stuck out his head. There, passing him by in quick succession, came several marvellous coaches emblazoned with noble coats of arms and pulled by flashy teams of horses.

"Cracking!" Darcy shouted, smiling and waving as the high-steppers trotted grandly past him, but the smile faded in the time it took the horses to disappear down the street. *Cracking.* Father would not approve of such a word, one among many that Darcy had acquired during this, his first term away at school. It was not that Mr. Darcy was a harsh parent. He was firm and formal, yes; but certainly nothing like the fathers in tales other boys at school had told. Some of the stories had been rather bloodcurdling, and he would have been tempted to disbelief were they not faithfully sworn to by their tellers. If his cousin, Richard Fitzwilliam, a year his senior and an old hand at Eton, also vouched for the lad, then he had, of course, no choice but to accept the tale.

Darcy thought of his cousin with warmth born of a life-long comradeship and, more recently, an immense debt of gratitude. He would most certainly have been sunk during his first term had it not been for Richard. He had plumbed Richard's knowledge of Eton the summer before during their rambles about Pemberley or Matlock. Well, plumbed as far as his cousin could be brought to talk about school on holiday. If not for Richard, he would have had little preparation for the unspoken rules, the snobbery, and the stark cruelty of the place. Even so, it was his cousin's tersely whispered promptings and frequent warnings that had enabled him to avoid most of the dangerous pitfalls that swallowed many a first-year student.

All in all, it had been a grand first term, and young Master Darcy was well satisfied with his standing among his fellows at its end. He had suffered a few drubbings—they could not all be avoided—but none had broken him. His own fists and Richard's had seen to that. Then, oddly enough, in their own way, so had the many years he'd had to deal with George Wickham. Nearly the same age, he and the son of his father's steward had been playmates in their infancy but increasingly uneasy companions as they grew older. George's propensity for trouble and his ability to deceive and deflect blame was extraordinary and, in Darcy's experience, quite dangerous. Many a time he had suffered his father's discipline or expressions of disappointment for something George had done. None of the lads at school had outshone George at this talent, and happily, Darcy's experience had enabled him to sidestep most such attempts. Yes, one of the best things about school had been that George was not there to plague him, and the only blemish upon this Christmas holiday was that George would also be returning from the respectable school to which Mr. Darcy had sent him.

A sharply worded shout from his coachman to another passing driver brought Darcy back to the present. He was returning home to Erewile House, the Darcy's London residence, for a few days before all the family set off for Derbyshire and Pemberley, their ancestral home. It was Christmas, and their traditional Pemberley celebration would close out this Year of Our Lord 1797. Christmas was always great fun at Pemberley, not only for the household but for all the surrounding neighbourhoods, whether rich or poor. His family's yearly largess ensured that no one would be in want. No, Mr. George Darcy was no Bluebeard or miser, but he was a man who held to the high standards of decorum and the *noblesse oblige* expected of men of his rank. Such a word as "cracking" that his son had acquired at school lay quite outside those lines. He would need to watch his tongue.

The carriage slowed yet more, and swinging around the corner of Grosvenor Square, it approached Erewile House where Samuel Coachman, the Darcy's driver, brought the horses to a halt. His oldest son James jumped from the box to open the door and let down the steps, but Darcy was too quick for him. Impatient to see his family, he threw the door open and leapt the few feet to the pavement. Although there was much he could not repeat to his father of what had occurred at school, there was still a great deal to share, and he could hardly wait to surprise him with all he had learned. Then, there was Mother to amaze…and the baby.

He raced up the steps, barely noting the Christmas greens decorating the doorway before he flung himself through the opening portal. "Master Darcy!" Witcher, Erewile House's butler, exclaimed as he stepped back from the entering whirlwind. "Welc–Oh, take care, sir!" His warning came too late. Darcy saw the looming black presence occupying a great deal of the hall only a moment before he ploughed straight into it. "Upfgh," the all too solid apparition exclaimed as Darcy's whole rushing weight hit him squarely and sent them both to the hall floor. For a few moments, all the boy could see was the ceiling, but that was soon obscured by the winged descent of the myriad papers the stranger's fall had sent flying. The breeze from the closing front door soon sent them winging randomly about the entire hall. Brushing away what landed on his face, Darcy lifted his ringing head. What, or rather, who had he tumbled over?

"Master Darcy! Are you all right?" Witcher clasped Darcy's hand, pulled him up, and dusted him off. The hall swam a bit before his eyes, but he soon came to focus on the figure lying at his feet A visitor? A servant? Whatever he was, he was dressed in unrelieved black, and his powdered and tied wig lay skewed over his forehead and into his eyes in so comical a fashion that Darcy could not but laugh.

"Mr. Hinchcliff, are you all right, sir? Can I help you?" Witcher asked, frowning at his young master before bending to assist the stranger.

"I am tolerable, Mr. Witcher, and have no need of assistance." A voice rumbled with so extraordinarily deep a resonance that the air itself vibrated. Darcy ceased laughing and stared in wonder as the man got his feet under him and slowly rose to his full height. He looked a giant! Long arms reached up to right the wig upon his head, revealing an enormous, high-bridged nose and eyes that seemed capable of discerning Darcy's innermost secrets. The boy gulped. A clergyman? A schoolmaster? Darcy felt a cold tremor of apprehension. His father must mean him to stick to his books over the holidays and, here, he had not only tumbled him over but then offended his new taskmaster before they had even begun!

"Master Darcy, I believe." the man's words pierced through Darcy's dread and disappointment at a holiday curtailed. "I am Hinchcliff, your father's new secretary, and you, sir, are awaited in the library." He peered down at him with a stern-jawed regard. "You will pardon me if I do not announce you, as I have now an unexpected task to complete; but I suggest you bestir yourself before your father comes into the hall in search of you." The giant turned then, and began retrieving the scattered letters and papers blanketing the floor.

"Yes, sir." Darcy's voice squeaked. Carefully, he picked his way through the debris to the stairs and slipped up to the first floor, his face burning from the incident but his mind relieved. There would be no lessons, only a glorious holiday with his family and cousins! He ran lightly to the library door stopping to straighten his waistcoat and pull down his cuffs before lifting his knuckles to tap out his arrival. As he did, a sound from within, a deep tremulous sigh that must be his father's, gave him pause. Puzzled, he leaned his ear against the door. A few footsteps and the sound of a chair scraping across the floor gave him to know that his parent was seated at his desk. Another sigh reached him through the door and then a sudden loud slam of a fist against wood and a cry of "Damn!" caused him to jump and withdraw a step. Drawing his brows together in consternation, Darcy stared at the door. What could be amiss with his father?

He stepped back and again cocked his ear to the library door, but no further indication of his father's temper escaped from behind it. Shrugging off his puzzlement, Darcy raised his fist once more and rapped his presence. A heartbeat of silence was followed by the command, "Enter." He pressed down the latch, only to have it leap out of his hand and his father appear in the open doorway.

"Fitzwilliam! You have come home at last!" His father's arm descended around his shoulders, and Darcy was pulled into the library and a brief embrace. Looking up into his father's countenance, he beheld evidence of a heavy weariness that overshadowed joy at his arrival. "My boy, how are you? Tell me of school." Mr. Darcy resumed his seat at the desk while his son took his accustomed position and stood tall before him.

"I am well, sir," he began. "Not too many bruises and none from the schoolmasters."

"Good, good," his father smiled. "And your marks, shall I be pleased when they arrive?"

"I have no concerns, Father. I was well prepared by Mr. Edridge and yourself and had no great difficulties. Cousin Richard was quite helpful as well"

"Richard was 'helpful,' eh?" Mr. Darcy snorted. "I can well imagine that scamp's help. It was not at lessons, I have no doubt."

"You underrate him, Father!" Darcy protested but then laughed at his father's knowing look. "He is a jolly good fellow to have for a cousin...or friend! He is really better at the books than you or my uncle might think. It is the exams that..." he trailed off into silence as a note of interest appeared on his father's face. Richard might not thank him for further revelations.

"Yes, well." Mr. Darcy looked speculatively at his son. "Richard is, fortunately, your uncle's to command and the authority to which he must answer. But," he added with a wry smile, "in general, I believe him to be merely high spirited." He paused. "Your uncle can not spare the time for Kent this year. Shall we ask his lordship if Richard may accompany us to Rosings in April?"

"Oh, yes, sir! That would be cracking!" The slang no sooner escaped him than Darcy blanched and bit his lip. He had sworn to watch his tongue not half an hour ago! Had his father noticed?

Mr. Darcy nodded and continued without reproach. "It shall be done." He sighed then and sank back in his chair, closing his eyes, the fingers of one hand working at his temple. Darcy watched this uncharacteristic display with silent concern. What could it be? Mr. Darcy's eyes returned to his son. His hand dropped and gripped the edge of his desk and he took a deep breath. "Now, I must trust you with some distressing news—a blow, really—but you are a young man now, Fitzwilliam, and know what is expected of a gentleman in regard to misfortune."

"Yes...Father." Darcy looked wonderingly at his parent, trying but failing to suppress a frisson of dread at the serious turn of his father's words and countenance. He straightened his shoulders even more, half expecting to hear them crack in the cold tension that gripped him. He waited, silent, watching as his father endeavoured to master a swell of rare, unmanly emotion.

Mr. Darcy rose from the desk and turned to the window overlooking the Square. He leaned stiffly against the sash, his eyes unseeing. "Your mother has not been well, my boy. The doctors…" He sighed again, raggedly. "The doctors are undecided concerning treatment, but on this they agree: that nothing, ultimately, may be done to cure her." He turned haunted, stricken eyes upon Darcy's blanched face. "We shall have her for a year, mayhap a little more, but certainly not two; and she will be in some—considerable—p-pain," he choked at the last, but recovered and stood straighter. "We must be brave and—"

"No! Father!" Darcy cut him off with a strangled cry. *Mother dying? Mother?* His stomach heaved and hollowed as if from a physical blow, and he staggered. *No, no, it could not be!*

"Fitzwilliam!" His father stepped toward him, a hand outstretched, but Darcy backed away, his eyes ablaze with tears, burning starkly in his bloodless face.

"W-when…" he gulped, his throat rebelling at speech. "When may I see her?"

"She expects you at the end of our interview." Mr. Darcy replied, swallowing hard as his son trembled.

So soon? Darcy's frame shook. *How was he…how could he?*

"She does not wish to speak of it nor to have her condition generally known. We must respect that, my son, and go on as before. Though every feeling cries out against it, Christmas…" he paused, unable to disguise the pain that forced another deep sigh. "We must continue with Christmas and do all we have ever done. I do not know how we can, but it is her wish, and so it shall be." Suddenly, he stepped to Darcy and grasped his shoulders. "We must not fail her in these things, Fitzwilliam. I hardly know how we shall bear it, but we must and for her sake. Promise…" He stopped and searched his son's face. "But I have said you are a young man, and so you are." He released him and waited for Darcy to look into his face. "Rather, give me your word," he demanded quietly. "Do I have your word that you will do as she asks, act as she wishes?"

Darcy looked away, his lip trembling as hot tears bathed his cheeks. How could his father demand this of him? It was impossible…fantastical! He screwed his eyes shut and wiped at them with the heels of his hands. *Mother!* His heart cried out. He felt sick, sick and weak as a baby, not the young man his father wanted him to be. He knew what was expected of him, what he must answer; but it was so very hard. He sniffed and cleared the lump from his throat, only to have it take up burning residence in his chest.

"Yes, sir," he answered, his voice hoarse. "You have my word…as a gentleman."

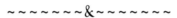

Darcy could still feel the weight of his father's hand upon his shoulder and the deep, vibrating sound of his "Well done, Fitzwilliam" as he quietly closed the library door. He walked down the hall a few paces before stopping. Fear and confusion overwhelmed him, and he leaned against the wall, unable to see or even think clearly. His father's final words, "Now, go to your mother," were a command he dare not postpone his mother must be awaiting him, the servants having certainly alerted her to his arrival. Her rooms were not visible from where he stood, but he peered down the empty hall ahead of him to the corner around which they lay and then looked back to the safety of the library door. His eyes welled up again. He was trapped, trapped between expectations that no lesson had yet taught him to fulfil. What was he to do or say once he actually faced his mother?

Stop crying like a baby! an inner voice sharply ordered. Darcy wiped again at his eyes and stood away from the wall. She certainly would not want tears. Should he try to smile or pretend that all was well? Should he even ask how she felt? *Oh, God!* he implored Heaven, *what do I do?* Heaven voiced no answer, nor did his conscience, save that he had delayed longer than his father would deem obedient. There was nothing for it but to go. Taking a deep breath, he continued slowly down the hall, stepping carefully to make as little sound to herald his approach as possible. What he heard instead was a softly pitched giggle that issued from around the corner. He stopped at the sound, frowning. *Who could–* There was another giggle, almost a shriek, and a little white cap, then a pair of dancing eyes peeked at him from around the corner.

"Georgiana!" Darcy scolded. "What are you doing there?" He strode to her and observed the leading strings trailing behind her. "Where is Nurse?" His sister looked up at him, all glee at escape gone. "Georgiana?" Her two year-old lips pursed at him, and a little frown creased her forehead, then just as suddenly cleared. "Fiss!" she cried and held up her arms to him. With a fleeting concern for his coat and neck cloth, he bent over and hoisted her up into his arms. "Fitz," he corrected her, but she only beamed at him and placed a moist kiss on his cheek.

"Hmph," he grunted and grimaced at her, only to receive a plump-handed pat on the spot. "Kiss," she informed him gravely.

"Yes, that is a kiss, my girl, but where is Nurse? You should not be wandering the house alone." Georgiana vouchsafed no opinion on that score but seemed content to settle into his arms and gaze at him fondly. Pulling the leading strings up into his bundle of the child and her skirts, he stepped around the corner. The hall to his mother's chamber was vacant, but her door was ajar. Georgiana must have come from there, slipping out of their mother's room when no one was looking.

"Back you go, Dolly, before you— Oh, too late!" A frantic Nurse appeared that moment at the door, observed her errant charge and her captor, and then hurried toward them both.

"Master Darcy, here you are...and with Miss. I'll just take the little moppet." She reached for Georgiana, but he forestalled her.

"No, let me take her in to Mother. She is not too tired for us both, is she?" Nurse looked doubtful, but Darcy insisted, not inclined to relinquish what he had quickly realized would be an excellent distraction.

"The mistress is very anxious to see you, sir," she replied slowly, eyeing the two of them. "I suppose the young miss might go back in, but you must call for me if she cries. I shall be right here in the hall."

"I will. Thank you, Nurse." Darcy resettled the baby on his hip and made for his mother's door before the little girl could display any inclination to cry and ruin his newly formed plan.

His mother's room was still the light and airy one of his memory, not the dark, fetid sickroom of his fears. Stepping into it that afternoon, he could detect nothing different from the countless other times he had done the same over his thirteen years. *Could his father have exaggerated his mother's illness?* She sat at her desk, her head bent to a letter which she dropped upon hearing his footstep.

"Fitzwilliam, you have come at last!" She looked up, smiling at him. It was then that he noticed the thinning of her face and the hint of pallor. "And with our naughty little run-away," she added affectionately.

"Fiss," Georgiana announced him to their mother and patted his cheek again. "Fiss here!"

"Yes, darling, Fitz is here." She rose, took her daughter from him and motioned that he should take a seat on the divan where they joined him. "I cannot tell you how happy we are that you are home, my dear. I…we, your father and I, have missed you dreadfully; although, I suspect you have been having a great adventure at school." She looked into his face expectantly. "Have you?"

Darcy returned her regard hesitantly and, in a subdued tone, replied, "Adventure, Mama? I think not. Rather, it has been lessons, exams, and a multitude of names and rules to learn."

"But, surely, it has not all been books and rules!" she persisted with a smile. "Your cousin would have seen to that! His father, my brother, was up to every lark at school, and Richard is more his father's son than Matlock will admit to anyone."

The idea of Uncle Matlock as a mischief-seeking school-boy was almost enough to make Darcy laugh, but not to-day, not with this crushing weight upon his heart that made him want to weep. "Richard was wonderful, Mama. He prevented me from committing stupid…well, more stupid mistakes than I did."

"I see," Lady Anne replied quietly.

"I did well at my studies," Darcy assured her, not certain what she "saw" but eager to make her proud and happy.

"And have you made any friends?"

"Yes, ma'm. Beginning to, I should say. Richard said not to go too fast in deciding. His set is a jolly bunch. I like them, but they are more...umm," he paused to find the least incriminating term, "lively than I."

Lady Anne patted his shoulder. "That is good advice, I dare say; but do not be too long in securing your own circle. You would not wish to be thought above your company or, heaven forbid, priggish."

"Mama!"

"Of course, you are not, and you are right to be careful," his mother cajoled, soothing the pride she had wounded. "But you are like your father in that you are very deliberate where so many are careless or do not see the point. It leads to misunderstandings that often are...troubling." She stopped and, lifting his chin with her free hand, placed a kiss upon his cheek. "Never mind; you will always be perfection itself in my eyes."

Georgiana, who had watched their conversation with interest, if not understanding, suddenly chortled and clapped her plump hands together. "Kiss! Mama kiss Fiss!"

"Yes, she did, Sweetling," Lady Anne held her daughter close. At first, it was a strong and tender embrace whose scope included himself, though he was not part of it; but as Darcy smiled at them, his mother seemed to wilt and the embrace become a thing shadowed by a kind of desperation.

"Mama, you are tired," he blurted out. "Let me call Nurse." He rose before she could answer and, striding to the door, summoned the woman. She came quickly.

"Here, my lady; let me take the little Miss. It is long past time for her bread and butter." Lady Anne stiffened, unused to her affairs being decided for her, but then her proud shoulders sagged and with a nod, she relinquished the child.

"There now," Nurse said as she settled the little girl on her hip. "Some nice bread and butter and a little Cambric tea from Cook and it shall be time for a nap. Can you say 'good-bye' to your mama and your brother?" Georgiana nodded. "Goo-bye," she lisped as she waved to them.

Darcy tugged at the edge of her skirts. "Good-bye, Dolly. I will see you soon." When they had left, he turned back to his mother. They must talk. As painful as it was, they must finally talk. She looked small and worn, two things he never in his life had associated with her. Almost as tall as his father, his mother had always appeared strong and vibrant to him. How could she have become ill, deathly ill, in the few months he had been away at school? "Mama," he began as he returned to her side, but she hushed him and took his long-fingered hands in hers.

"My dear, dear son," she sighed as she gripped his hands tightly. "You have seen your father?"

"Yes, Mama," he whispered hoarsely. "He...he told me that you are ill."

"More than ill, my own." She brought his hands to her lips and kissed them. "I am dying." Her voice faltered. Darcy choked, tears leaping to his eyes. Vehement denials pressed against his heart and lips, but she had declared it to be true. It must be true. What was left for him to do save what he had promised?

"W-what...how...tell me, Mama," he stuttered miserably. "I do not know."

"None of us know, Fitzwilliam, until it comes to us; and then we learn. I am learning," she whispered, "as is your dear father. You shall, as well. Meanwhile," she spoke now with firmness, "we shall go on as we have always meant to go until it is...impossible. And, until that time comes, we shall not burden others with it. Do you understand, my son?"

"I promised Father."

"I am sure you did. Now you must promise me." She closed her eyes as she pulled him into an embrace and tried to explain herself. "I do not wish false cheer any more than long faces, Fitzwilliam. Nor do I wish you to pretend that the facts are not such as they are. That would be foolish and, perhaps, even wicked. What I want is that this dying will not be the primary fact of our lives. I want us all to live while I am yet alive. That is what I ask of you."

Darcy knew he would always remember the smell of her, the beat of her heart and the soft flow of her breath as she held him. Reluctantly, he drew back from the sweet haven, but his mother retained his hands. He looked into her face and with all the love in his heart gave his word. "I will, Mama. I promise."

Chapter 2

Society had already seen London thin of company before Darcy had arrived home from school. Therefore, with every reason to leave and preparations for the journey all but completed, his father directed that the family set off for Pemberley without delay and Erewile House be closed until Parliament was again in session. The next day the servants' parlour was cleared for the household staff's Christmas dinner to be followed by a night of merriment before the family departed. Darcy, along with his mother and father, attended the opening of the party, his father presenting the upper servants with their Christmas gifts and entrusting Witcher with the distribution of the family's appreciation to the lower staff. Mr. Darcy toasted them and the evening, wishing them a very merry Christmas and year to come, before he and Lady Anne retired above stairs and left the staff to their dancing and bowl of Christmas punch.

Darcy almost wished to stay behind. The smells of the greenery combined with Cook's marvellous pastries and cakes were intoxicating to a boy fresh from a term of school fare. To his embarrassment, his stomach had actually growled upon his first whiff. Of course, he could not stay. They would be home at Pemberley in a few short days, and Pemberley's cook was every bit the equal of the artist at Erewile House. Darcy knew from experience there would be nothing to regret. Nevertheless, it was with undisguised delight that he found a plate of his favourite sweets next to his bedside candle after bidding his parents goodnight.

The following day they were off, travelling now in the great coach whose springs had been lately replaced to make the trip as smooth as possible for Lady Anne. His mother directed both he and his father not to tax her with their solicitude at every bump or jolt. They did not; although, it tore at Darcy's heart to see how bravely she bore them. Gripping Aristotle's *Ethics,* whose last chapters had bee assigned for next term, and hiding behind the pages was, he found, the only way he could abide by his mother's wishes.

Their trip was uneventful, save for the few hours on the second day that Darcy was allowed to sit up with Samuel in the box and observe a master at the whip and reins.

"How do you do it, Samuel?" Darcy ached to imitate the expert manner that the family's coachman handled the yards of whip, tickling the leader's ear and then swirling the end to wrap elegantly around the handle.

"That would be tellin', now wouldn't it, young master." The coachman smiled at him and winked to his son James on Darcy's other side.

"Telling what?"

"A tradesman's secret, a secret of the brotherhood, so to speak."

"Brotherhood? There is a brotherhood of coachmen?" Darcy looked at him curiously. "I have never heard of such a thing!"

"Well, yer not supposed to be knowin' such," he declared gruffly but then seemed to relent. "But I know yer a close lad and won't tell summat you've sworn not to tell. You do so swear?" Samuel demanded as he peered down at him.

"Oh, yes, of course," Darcy promised. He glanced over at James, who nodded his solemn approval.

"Well then, next summer, when yer home from school," Samuel promised, "we'll see what may be done about inductin' you."

"Into the brotherhood?" Darcy asked, not quite sure how far this unexpected good fortune extended.

"Into the first ranks only, young sir. It will likely take the whole summer to get far enough to call you a cub." Samuel eyed him with a measuring look. "If you will practice, that is."

"Oh, I will!" he assured them, grinning from one to the other. "This is famous!"

~ ~ ~ ~ ~ ~ ~ & ~ ~ ~ ~ ~ ~ ~

They arrived home the following day. Darcy's hopes for the holiday were not certain until they reached Lambton, the village that lay five miles west of Pemberley House. There the several inches of snow in the fields and ice on the pond that greeted them promised a Christmas of sledding, skating, and general sport enough to satisfy the desires of any young man. Leaving the village behind, the coach traced the path of the Ere River until it wound north of the road that took them to the gates of Pemberley. The drive through Pemberley's park was designed to be taken slowly, each turn in the road created to present a new aspect to delight the traveller and heighten expectations for what was to come. For Darcy, however, anxious to be freed from the confines of the coach, it was tedious beyond belief; but the misty smile it brought to his mother's face persuaded him to hold his peace and force himself to sit still.

The horses' gaits changed at the exact moment that Darcy heard Samuel's whip crack, and he knew that they had gained the sweeping approach that led down to Pemberley's door. He sat up closer to the edge of the seat and tried to see around the coach and horses to the pond, but the vehicle dipped and swayed to a faster rhythm now, making it impossible. He glanced in exasperation to his parents only to see his father take his wife's hand. "My dear," he questioned softly, "shall I tell them to slow?"

"No, I am well enough, Mr. Darcy, and longing to be home," she answered him, her voice tired and strained. "Do not stay the horses."

"As you wish," he agreed, but his glance at Darcy was apprehensive even as he stroked her hand.

"Mama," he began, attempting to distract them both, "have you ever noticed how well Samuel wraps his whip?"

Lady Anne's lips curved into a tight smile. "No, I cannot say that I have," she replied, her brows raised in invitation to more conversation despite the obvious pain she was battling.

"Oh, he is quite the best whip in the country...for a coachman. Do you not think so, Father?"

"Undoubtedly," his sire agreed, a light of amusement entering his eyes. "He taught me, you know."

"Truly?" Was his father part of the brotherhood then? Darcy looked at him speculatively but could come to no conclusion, for at that moment, the coach slowed and stopped before Pemberley's front stairs. In only seconds, the great doors of the house were flung open. Reynolds, Pemberley's butler, and his army of footmen surged down the stairs and around the coaches and other vehicles in the entourage. The stable lads appeared, seemingly from nowhere, to welcome back their equine charges, attacking the harnessing and leading them away to a well earned measure of grain.

"Mr. Darcy, My Lady, welcome home!" Reynolds bowed to his master and mistress as soon as one of his subordinates had opened the coach door and let down the steps.

"Happy Christmas, Reynolds," Mr. Darcy replied as he rose and descended first in order to help his wife. "Are you ready for your mistress?"

"Oh, yes, sir. Mrs. Reynolds prepared everything exactly as your letter required." Reynolds turned then to the coach's other occupants. "May I help you, Ma'am?" He extended his arm, which Lady Anne took as well as that of her husband's on her other side. Slowly, she descended to the pavement before Pemberley's stairs.

"Thank you, Reynolds," her ladyship nodded and leaned upon her husband. "Mr. Darcy has me in charge now."

Reynolds stepped away and bowed again before turning to his young master. "Master Darcy!" he exclaimed as the boy rattled down the coach steps. "You have grown quite tall since the summer!"

Darcy grinned into the butler's lively face. Reynolds had always been one of his favourite people at Pemberley. "I believe I have! Happy Christmas, Reynolds!"

"And to you, sir," he replied as they walked into the hall. "Mrs. Reynolds charged me to tell you that Cook will have something special for you in the breakfast room as soon as you are settled." He then lowered his voice, "I expect that your parents may wish to rest before taking any refreshment. I am sure there can be no expectation that you should wait upon them." He gave the boy a wink and left the hall.

Turning his eyes to the stairs, Darcy saw that his parents were still ascending them, his father with an arm about his wife's waist as they slowly assayed each step. He could easily recall his mother taking those stairs with quicker, lighter steps. Her slow, laboured procession now was yet another reminder of what lay ahead and a further cut to his young heart.

"Master Darcy!" Darcy looked around to find the owner of the warm voice.

"Mrs. Reynolds," he smiled. "Happy Christmas!"

"Happy Christmas, indeed! Did Mr. Reynolds not give you my message?" The eyes of Pemberley's housekeeper rested upon him briefly before glancing up the stairs behind him. She softly clucked her tongue but then directed her attention wholly upon him again. "Did he not tell you Cook has something that requires your attention in the breakfast room?"

"He did, ma'am. I was just on my way," his voice trailed off as he looked over his shoulder, unable to stop himself from searching out his parents' slow progress on the stairs. They had paused for his mother to catch her breath. He looked back at Mrs. Reynolds, his face taut with the effort to disguise his fear. She had followed his gaze, but when he turned back to her, her eyes snapped back to his face. Her tongue clucked again.

"Come, young master; I would not be surprised if Cook's treats have yet to leave the kitchen. Like as not, they will taste better the nearer they are to the oven." She cast him a reassuring smile that was transformed into a yet broader one when his sister and her nurse appeared in the doorway behind him. "Miss Georgiana!" she cried. "Is that my little poppet, then?" She patted Darcy's shoulder, gently urging him to the kitchen below before bustling over to greet the newcomers.

He heard his sister's insistent call of "Fiss!" on his way to the kitchen but did not pause to do more than wave to her. Cook's treats and the warmth of Pemberley's kitchen awaited him, and after the cold and strained trip from London, the delicious normalcy of both sounded splendid, indeed.

Later, his stomach warmly content from the culinary welcome afforded by Cook and the kitchen servants, Darcy slipped up the stairs, intent upon gaining the safety of his rooms. He carefully made his way past his parents' chambers, unwilling to be drawn into the suffering that lay behind its door by a summons precipitated by the sound of his passing. Opening his own door, he ran straightway to the windows of his bedchamber that faced out upon the pond and the snow-drifted hills that swept down from the Park. The ribbon of gravel that was the drive was the only disturbance in the crystalline expanse. The snow lay glinting under an impossibly blue sky. The pond, already cleared of its cover, awaited him, as was all the familiar, consoling beauty of Pemberley. He sat on the broad sill and drank it in, vista to vista, infinitely grateful that home, at least, had not changed.

~ ~ ~ ~ ~ & ~ ~ ~ ~ ~

Dinner that night was largely a silent affair. Lady Anne did not come down, and Darcy's father kept his own counsel for much of it, his eyes pools of sadness that barely comprehended the food before them. Darcy chanced quick glances at him, hoping for the appearance of something of the father he knew. He would not ask after his mother, he decided. Her absence and his father's pain made that polite exercise only an occasion for the further eroding of their tenuous composure.

26

The unusual silence, broken only by the clink of silver against china and the swish and step of the servants as they attended them, began to work on him. Darcy shifted in his chair and straightened, seeking relief from the tension in such a way that would not draw his father's notice. He did not but the dining room door behind his father opened just then, and Darcy looked up to see Reynolds standing in the doorway surveying the room. The servants all stiffened and paused, unsure what was causing their superior to shake his head in such a manner. Only Darcy dared to follow Reynolds gaze which fell squarely upon his father's back and then shifted to him. Reynolds' lips pursed before falling into a solicitous smile as he approached the dining table. Motioning the other servants to continue with their duties, he presented himself to his master.

"Excuse me, sir," he began and bowed.

Darcy's father looked at him in surprise, then in trepidation. "Reynolds! What is it? Her ladyship?" He made to rise from the table.

"No, no, sir. Her ladyship is resting comfortably," Reynolds assured them. "I merely wish to ascertain whether there is anything amiss with dinner. Cook stands ready to prepare something more to your taste, if you wish it." He glanced over to Darcy, then back to his master, his face an open invitation to them to express their desires.

Mr. Darcy's face flushed slightly and some animation returned to his features. "No, Reynolds, this is perfectly good fare. I just do not seem to have much appetite this evening. Perhaps, Master Darcy would prefer something else."

"No, sir," Darcy responded to the combined regard of both men. "This is very good, Reynolds. Much better than school," he murmured. "But, I am not so hungry, either."

"Very good, Master Darcy; I shall have the plates removed. Shall dessert be held or—"

"Oh, no, Reynolds!" Darcy blurted out before thinking. He coloured at his father's arched brow but relaxed a bit when Reynolds winked at him from behind his master. "That is, I should very much like dessert."

"Why 'very much'?" his father asked, his features softening. "Do you know what it is?"

"Yes, sir. I visited the kitchen earlier, and Cook said that since I had been away so long to school he was making my favourite to remind me what good food tastes like." Actually, Cook had said something so astringent about the food at school that Darcy deemed it appropriate to paraphrase. Even so, his father chuckled, and Reynolds' lips twitched.

"Well, then," Mr. Darcy said with a smile, "I am not one to stand in Cook's way when he has a point to make, especially when it concerns dessert. Reynolds," he commanded with a light in his eye, "bring the dessert—for both of us."

"Very good, sir," Reynolds replied with mock gravity. Bowing to both, but adding another wink to his young master, he straightened and walked out the door like a man who had accomplished his mission.

Darcy grinned sheepishly up at his father, hoping that his impetuous incivility to Reynolds had broken through the fortress of his father's sadness enough to continue the evening in a semblance of their old companionship. "Father," he began, "are you part of the Brotherhood?" The question of his sire's place in the world of whipsters was one that had plagued him at school, long before Samuel Coachman's shared confidence. He'd asked Richard what he knew of his father's standing, only to be vaguely assured by his cousin that "Uncle Darcy is a rare one" and took second to no boy's father.

"The Brotherhood?" Mr. Darcy replied, taking a nut from a bowl and cracking it open. "Which Brotherhood might this be?"

"Samuel Coachman's Brotherhood."

"Samuel's?" his father queried, his brow wrinkled, then cleared. "Ah, I remember now. No, not the Brotherhood of Coachmen; that is not for gentlemen."

Darcy reached for a nut and tried to crack it open with his hands as his father had done. "The Four-And-Go Club?" he asked with some hesitancy. "Some of the lads at school boasted that their fathers were Four-And-Goers. Only the best whips can be members."

His father slid the nutcracker over to him without comment and waited for the loud crack before answering with his own question. "What have you heard of the Goers, Fitzwilliam?"

Here was dangerous ground! What he'd heard had been exciting: mad dashes across country, fantastic wagers won and lost, the heroic feats of legendary horses, but some other things had been rather shocking. "Well, sir," he began carefully, "a candidate must have first passed a test of driving skill even to be considered. It is rather exacting."

"Yes, it is," his father agreed with a nod. "What else?"

"His Highness, the Prince of Wales was rejected for membership and threatened the club's officers, but they stood firm. That was rather brave; was it not?"

"Perhaps." Mr. Darcy reached for another nut, cracked it, and shared it with his son. "Do you think it was brave?"

"I thought so when I heard the story," Darcy responded. "The other lads declared it was a topping thing to have done." He paused, his brow wrinkling. "Was it not bad form for the Prince to threaten them?"

"Yes, it was, Fitz, very bad form. But was it brave for the officers to have wounded the pride of a very powerful man for the sake of a driving club?" He cocked his head. "What might have become of them or their families?"

"I don't know, sir," Darcy confessed after a short consideration and looked down at his hands, away from his parent's intent gaze. The clatter of the dining room door opening put a pause to their conversation. Darcy looked up at the plate in the footman's grasp and followed its descent to the table in front of him. The baked apple pudding looked absolutely marvellous, the puff paste a golden brown, and it smelled even better. The anticipation must have been written plainly across his face, for his father laughed and told him to tuck in before his jaw hit the table. They ate in companionable silence for the first several bites. Then, Mr. Darcy relaxed against the back of his chair and turned his attention once more to his son. Darcy grinned back at him between spoonfuls but concentrated most intently upon his dessert.

"Clearly, we will have no worthwhile conversation until you have finished becoming one with your dessert," he addressed Darcy affectionately. "Therefore, I will assume the burden of it and begin with an answer, proceed to a confession, and end, as any good father should, with a caution. Whether I have made my case, you must decide and order your life accordingly." He motioned a servant to pour his coffee, amended it himself with sugar and cream, and sat back in his chair once more to regard his son. "To begin—yes, I was a member of the Four-And-Go Club."

"Oh, Father!" Darcy cried, his face alighting with pride and some relief. What a grand thing he would have to boast of when he returned to school! The Four-And-Goers' exploits were the stuff of legend and the envy of less proficient whipsters the country over. Membership was extremely selective, and the test for admittance was said to require the most exacting bits of driving imaginable, a team of four impeccably matched and fearless examples of horseflesh, and a good deal of raw nerve. Its prestige was enormous; witness, that His Highness had petitioned for membership. The Prince's failure to qualify and resultant tantrum remained the prime example of "bad form" whispered among schoolboys even to the present day. But, why had he not known this before or seen any indication of his father's expertise in their drives together?

Mr. Darcy responded to his son's look of adulation with a wry self-conscious smile. "You may wonder why I have never told you of this or even mentioned the Goers. That is where the confession I mentioned enters our conversation."

Darcy looked curiously at his father, intensely interested in his extraordinary revelation. At the same time, he could not but be conscious of the fact that his father was speaking to him differently than he had before he had left for school, and with it, a new sense of maturity burned proudly in his chest. "Please, go on, sir."

"I must also tell you that I was, in my youth, a founding member of the Goers."

"One of the Originals?" Darcy could scarcely believe it; his esteem for his father grew exponentially. His father, an Original! The beginning of the Goers was shrouded in a mystery still perpetuated by the current membership. The founders, or "Originals" as they had been dubbed, were never named and only identified by the aliases with which they had christened themselves. While the membership were known to each other, the Originals, it was said, never appeared among them unmasked. Darcy fairly shivered with the wonder of it. *His father!*

"Yes, an Original," Mr. Darcy affirmed and then grimaced, "and as foolish and hot-tempered as anyone in that day. Fitzwilliam, I know it sounds terribly exciting–and it was, for a time–but I would remind you that this is a confession." He reached for another nut and rolled it back and forth between his palms. "As you have probably already deduced, I was one of the officers who rejected His Highness's petition for membership. We were a devil-may-care set and demanded driving of the most reckless sort to qualify for membership. We were, at least, perfectly sober for our races; it was an absolute rule and one with which all the Originals knew the Prince incapable of compliance. For that reason alone he should have been rejected; but he was a rather ham-fisted driver as well. So, it was in derision of his driving that we, in our pride, spaded him."

Darcy nodded his understanding. It was not an uncommon way of voting on membership into a group: a heart card was laid down for acceptance, a spade for rejection. The higher the value of the card, the greater was the intensity of feeling being expressed for or against the candidate.

"Doubtless, you have heard somewhat concerning His Highness's reaction to our dismissal of his suite. It might have gone badly, very badly, had his agents ever discovered who we were. I tell you honestly, our pride and bravado lasted less than a fortnight before it was brought home to us how dangerous it is to enrage a monarch–or a future one. A way would have been found to bring down our families in disgrace, endangering all of our futures for nothing more than the temporary pleasure of sitting in judgement upon one above us in station and rank because he could not drive four ill-tempered beasts to our satisfaction." A thrill of excitement at his father's story, heightened by the dread his sire meant him to feel, raced up Darcy's back. Mr.

Darcy checked a sigh at his son's excited shiver and continued. "Was it brave? No, Fitzwilliam, it was not. It was as
foolish a thing as we might ever have done, save for that
with which I will conclude—the caution."

Darcy pushed his empty plate away, at one and the same
time burning to know and dreading to hear what could be
worse in his father's eyes than the disgrace he had nearly
visited upon his family. Of all things, the possibility of
disgrace was held as a delicately balanced sword above the
heads of every boy of his class, serving to curb all but the
most dissolute in the chase after excitement or dominion.
Every temptation was weighed against it.

"Yes, Father?" he finally replied, signalling his readiness.

Mr. Darcy rolled the nut between his palms once again
and then laid it back in the dish. "About four months after
rejecting His Highness's application, we were approached
by another, a young lord not even a year out of University
who fancied himself equal to the test. He was a very like-
able young man, amiable, gentlemanly in almost every
instance except in one—his passion for racing. In becoming
a Goer, he considered that he would prove himself up to
any challenge. I, for one, liked him immensely until it came
to that subject, upon which he became exceedingly tire-
some. The Originals, myself included, decided that, after a
severe test of driving skill with impossible time constraints
to teach him some humility, we would card him into the
club.

"I shall never forget that morning. It was not yet light
when we accompanied him out of the inn and boosted him
up to the driver's seat. His face was as white as a gander's
wing, though his eyes were bright and hard in the torchlight
as he wound the lines about his gloved hand and uncurled
his whip. I remember thinking as I watched him that he

would never acknowledge the absurdity of our test but would press all to the uttermost. How I wish I would have stopped him, confessed our plan! But the impression was only a momentary one, and none of us thought he would fail to exercise reason even as he courted the danger.

"The test began with the first ray of dawn. At the crack of his whip, his team sprang forward, and our whoops spurred him on to the first checkpoint. He made the first and then the second, but later that morning, a boy from a farm near the third rode into the yard on the checkpoint observer's horse, calling for help."

Darcy sat very still, barely breathing, and completely unable to take his eyes from his father's face. He could guess what was to come and did not want to hear it. He blinked several times and swallowed hard. His father nodded his understanding but, leaning forward, continued.

"We found a physician and, bundling him onto one of the member's horses, set out after our young lord. We arrived only moments before it was all over. He… he had taken a corner above a ravine far too fast and overset his phaeton. It rolled on him as he went down." He paused to swallow the catch in his voice before continuing. "The sight of his broken body and the fearful confusion on his face as death rushed to claim him is something I can never forget. The fact that I had a part in what had happened to him is an awful regret I live with to this very day."

His father reached again for a nut from the bowl and swiftly cracked it, giving him half. "It was a horrible thing and painful to confess to you, Fitzwilliam, but I wish you to know that your father is a fallible man, and, as it is in man's nature, it is inevitable that you shall be so as well. My hope in telling you this is that, in your own battles with failings and foolishness, you will not be as heedless as I or suffer such pangs for them."

Mr. Darcy fell silent and looked earnestly at his son in a wordless request for assurance that Darcy understood the moral. Shivering with the horror of the story as well as the burden his father bore, Darcy signalled his understanding but could not think what to say.

His father pushed back his chair and rose briskly, motioning Darcy to do likewise. Then, putting his hands on his son's shoulders, he gave him a loving shake. Darcy smiled and hesitantly asked, "What now, sir? Are you still—"

"A member? I resigned as an officer on the day of his lordship's funeral and have, since meeting your mother, been a member emeritus only." He peered at his son, and then continued, "Which does not mean that I have forgotten how to drive to an inch." Darcy grinned up at him, and his father smiled back before dropping his hands and assuming a more formal pose, his brows cocked as he measured his son's stature. Darcy threw back his shoulders, anxious that his father's examination would not find him wanting. "Hmm," Mr. Darcy murmured as if coming to a decision which required some pondering.

"Sir?"

"Although I may be a bit out of practice, Fitzwilliam, I believe I still retain enough skill to teach you the finer points of how a gentleman whip handles a team." He laughed at the sudden brightening of his son's countenance. "And I also believe that this summer is not too soon to start!"

Chapter 3

Darcy's second morning home at Pemberley dawned with the promise of a high blue sky, issuing anew the call to sport and adventure that had tugged at him since his arrival. Throwing off his bed-clothes, he hurried to his windows. Using the side of his fist, he rubbed away at the frost whose sharp edges caught at the sun but together obscured his view of snow-covered hill, wood, and pond. Oh, there was so much that might be enjoyed if only his cousins were here!

A letter from his uncle, their father, Lord Matlock, had arrived late the previous evening with information concerning his family's descent upon Pemberley. Breaking the seal, his father had read it out to him, imitating the droll tone of its author:

Darcy,

My dearest companion and helpmeet desires that I write you straightaway concerning our impending arrival that you may be well prepared for the cutting up of any peace you may have hoped to enjoy this holy season. Lady Matlock, myself, and our pair of hell-hounds will arrive a week from Friday, if it please you, in the late afternoon. I say, "if it please you," only as a matter of formality, for my lady will not be deterred from Christmas at Pemberley if it please you or not, and the boys have threatened to abscond with my two best horses should the carriage not be ready at the crack of dawn. There you have it. I expect the best from your cellar as recompense.

Your obedient servant and slave to my family's
every wish,
Matlock

So, it would not be until the following week that he could hope to see D'Arcy and Richard unless they did sneak their father's prize horses out of the stables and ride ahead. Such an event, he thought, was only a high-spirited threat and not likely serious. Lord Matlock was a man whose displeasure Darcy would not wish to court. He derived great pleasure from contemplating the absurd in his fellow man and neither of his sons were spared his barbed wit. Richard was becoming like him, having lately taken to calling his parents "Pater" and "Mater" just to hear his father's annoyed snort. But he was still loathe to press him to the point of a serious need for discipline and often spoke to Darcy of his horror of incurring it. Still, Richard and his elder brother were lively and adventurous lads who tested their sire's temper far more that Darcy would dare or even desire to try. Fortunately, their adventures were not grounded in determined roguery but, more often than not, in the pursuit of honest fun which occasionally tipped over the boundary of what their father deemed prudent. Darcy could hardly wait for them to arrive!

A low growl from his stomach hastened him from the window to the clothespress. It was much too early for breakfast, but there would undoubtedly be something to stave off hunger standing fragrant and delicious on Cook's table in the kitchen. Dressing hurriedly, Darcy slipped out his chamber door and moved silently through the hall and down the several sets of stairs leading to the kitchen. As he drew near, the smells escaping from that culinary shrine waxed comforting and enticing and entirely irresistible.

"Ahhh, 'tis a great pity and breaks my heart, so it does." The voice of one of the older kitchen servants drifted out the door. Darcy stopped short of the entrance and held his breath. Several quiet murmurs followed in reply.

"At least she be home and be a-stayin' 'til the end here, where she's loved," said another. "Not in Lun'un...they's cold folk in Lun'un." Another chorus of murmurs arose in strong assent to the character of that distant city.

"Likely, how she took ill," a third voice put in. "Never held with Lun'un nor any city, come to that." A short pause ensued. "I feel for all of 'um: my lady carryin' on so brave, the master..." The voice trailed off in a sigh.

"It ain' right!" cried another. "How many there be it would bless the world if they was takin' out of it! An' if the way be through sufferin'? Well, folk would say it was deserved and the judgement o' God for their bold wickedness. But, oh, my lady..." A sob choked the speaker.

Out in the dark corridor, Darcy pressed his fist to his lips, stifling a whimper born of gathering sorrow with the fresh sting of indignation that gripped his chest. Why? Why? The servant was right! Even he could name some whose certain wickedness merited calamity. Why should they live and prosper while his own mother–

"Hush, now," soothed the old servant. "Sorrowin' for her ladyship and the family is one thing. Those be tears His Own Self will one day wipe away. Folk callin' down judgements be another."

"What are you skulking out here for?" boomed a familiar voice behind him. "Spying on the servants, Darcy?" George

Wickham appeared from out of the dark passageway and slipped around him, jostling him slightly before he stepped into the full light falling through the kitchen door. "I'm hungrier for food than gossip myself!" He smirked at Darcy, then stepped inside. "What's for breakfast, Peg?"

Wickham. A flush warmed Darcy's face, but he had no choice save to follow his former playmate into the kitchen. The only son of his father's steward and just months younger than himself, Wickham had been his companion since childhood. In the beginning, when they were quite young, Wickham had been jolly fun, but other times were not so pleasant to recall. Darcy's mind drifted to a particularly painful memory...

"Fitzwilliam, that pony was discovered locked in his box, lathered, and blown! How could you treat the poor beast in such a manner?"

"Father, I didn't–

"Do not, Fitzwilliam, do not, I beg you, insult me or demean yourself with false denial. A man takes responsibility for his actions, no matter the penalty."

"But, Father, I–"

His father held up his hand, cutting him off. Then, reaching into his waistcoat pocket, he withdrew something. "I had hoped you would honour me with the truth one gentleman owes another without resorting to proof."

His father's tone made his vitals shrivel in disbelieving fear. *Proof?*

What proof could there possibly be for something he hadn't done? Besides, he loved his pony and would never mistreat him. Surely, Father knew that!

"This was found on the stable floor this morning." His father opened his hand, revealing a small, brown button.

He looked from the button to his father's stern, disappointed countenance. "A button?" he croaked, his throat tightening even as the circle of incrimination drew close around him.

His father's face fell, first into something like sorrow, then into anger. "You insist on playing the charade through! So be it!" He turned, strode to a chair and snatched up something lying on the seat. "Will you also deny that this is yours?" He held out a coat, a riding coat that was undeniably his; and there, on the front, the torn cloth and empty place in a row of buttons, small, brown buttons that exactly matched the one in his father's other hand.

It had been Wickham, of course. Wickham had been his daily companion and the leader in their play from the start. No one else would have dared to ride his pony or been so careless of it when he'd finished, or for that matter, been so clever to leave evidence against him. Even so, it had been rare that any blame for high spirits or misbehaviour was laid upon George. He should have known from the look on the boy's face when the pony first arrived, but they'd been only eight years old. He had not yet learned the power of envy. And now the servants thought he was spying! Darcy shrugged to himself. He was a young man and gone to school. His former degree of companionship with Wickham had cooled, and now it must be replaced by a relationship appropriate to their respective stations. Darcy had no illusions that this adjustment would be easy.

"Master Darcy! Good morning to you, young sir." The servants' greetings were open and warm as tears and sighs were quickly wiped away and shoulders were straightened to the tasks at hand. "You must be hungry," Peg, the undercook, asserted as her gaze travelled from Darcy to Wickham and back. "My, but the two of you have growed in the time you been gone to school. It must be what boys do," she said, shaking her head and motioning toward the table, "for it could no be the food!"

Darcy grinned and sat down at the end of the monstrous kitchen board that ran the length of the room. Wickham made to do the same, but Peg frowned him off. He hesitated a moment, quirking a brow at Darcy, silently inviting him to overrule Peg. When Darcy did not immediately do so, he laughed as if he knew precisely what Darcy was about and turned to the other end of the table. Darcy glanced at him as he sauntered away, unable to dismiss the prickly feeling creeping up his back. How was it that Wickham always seemed to gain the upper hand and make him feel mean-spirited in the bargain?

A plate heavy with food descended onto the table from behind him, banishing all philosophy to the kitchen's dark corners. "Peg, this is absolutely marvellous!" Darcy cried at the sight of the mound of savoury bacon and fresh bread. Soon, a crock of butter and a bowel of orange marmalade joined it, followed by a mug of tea, and containers of sugar and milk.

"It should keep you from faintin' until yer father coomes down," Peg declared, a great smile on her plain face. "Now, tuck in!" She waved her hand at the food and returned to her early morning tasks. Darcy gladly obeyed.

The food at Eton was plain and nourishing, claimed the schoolmasters, fit for encouraging the mind to apprehend the sublime and the body to harden for service to King and Country. Plain it most certainly was, but the assertion of nourishing, in Darcy's opinion, was highly suspect. Even so, the amount wouldn't satisfy the pangs of a cat, assuming anyone would be able to convince that animal to accept the school's dishes as provender.

A flurry of steps and conversation from the hall resolved itself into Mrs. Reynolds and Nurse. Nurse dropped him a curtsy after her startled "Oh!" upon realizing it was he at the table. "Excuse me, Master Darcy! I'm just about getting a tray for Miss." At his nod, she hurried off, but Mrs. Reynolds lingered.

"Mrs. Reynolds?" Darcy pushed his plate away and began to stand.

"No, no, my boy! Sit and eat," she admonished him with a smile. "Although, I suppose I should no longer 'my boy' you," she sighed. "For my part, it should be 'Master Darcy' and I merely 'Reynolds' now that you are a young gentleman at school."

"But then, how should I call for your husband, ma'am' Darcy grinned, "if you are both 'Reynolds'? If it pleases you, I should like to continue as before."

"If it pleases me?" She laughed lightly. "No, sir; if it pleases *you*, I shall remain 'Mrs.' and that is as it should be." She smiled down into his eyes. Darcy nodded again and pulled his plate back in front of him. The marmalade glistened only slightly more than the rich, thick butter that was begging to slather the fresh bread with delight. Darcy picked up his knife.

Some quick steps from the hall were followed by the entrance of his mother's maid into the kitchen. The concern upon her face was obvious as she scanned the room for help. Her eyes alighting on Peg, she let out a small sigh of relief. "Peg!" Peg looked up from her work and, seeing the lady's maid, immediately dusted her hands and came forward.

"What is it, Miss? A tray for her ladyship?"

"Yes," replied Miss Barrows, her voice uncertain and strained, "soon, but she asks for a hot poultice first. I'm fearful–"

"There now," Peg brushed the maid's arm and indicted Darcy sitting at the table. "A poultice is no trouble, Miss, and then some nice tea and toast. Some marmalade as well? Her ladyship is right proud of Pemberley's marmalade." Peg drew Miss Barrows off deeper into the kitchen while Darcy studiously pretended not to notice. After another bite, he stole a frightened look up at Mrs. Reynolds, whose gaze followed the two servants before glancing back down at him.

"We must all be brave, Master Darcy, brave for her," she whispered firmly, "and not allow our fears to overpower us. For, what use may we be to her if we are undone?"

A tear hovered at the corner of his eye, but Darcy blinked and commanded it away. "Yes, Mrs. Reynolds."

"Now," the housekeeper's brisk tone signalled another topic entirely. "I understand that Lord and Lady Matlock and your cousins are to arrive next week. That should be jolly fun for you, I daresay. How shall you prepare for them, I wonder?"

Oh! He hadn't considered his responsibilities as host to his cousins beyond the sport to be had out of doors. If the weather were not agreeable, other activities than those contrived in Richard's keen imagination would be needed. A visit to his old playroom and, perhaps, the attic storerooms was in order.

"Thank you, Mrs. Reynolds. I shall see to it directly."

"There's a good lad," she beamed at him and rose to her own many responsibilities as housekeeper to the great house of Pemberley.

At the other end of the table, Wickham stood up and, following the plate he slid down the board, came to a stop opposite Darcy. "Sorry," he said as he sat down. "About your mother." Darcy murmured an inchoate response of gratitude for George's polite motion, hoping no more would follow. It was too raw a thing. He need not have worried, for George had other things on his mind. "Good lord, but am I glad to be back. I don't know what they feed you at Eton, Darcy, but what we're given at St. Jude's isn't fit for swine. Do you think your father would send me to another – "

"I couldn't say, George." Darcy stopped him and grimaced. "If you've spoken to your father– "

"He won't hear a word against St. Jude's. 'Mr. Darcy's choice is better 'an you have any right to hope for.'" George imitated his father's rough country brogue. "So, if I'm to escape the rat hole, I must rely upon you, old man. Just a word."

Old man? Darcy's eyes narrowed. That was coming a bit strong! Did George fancy himself admitted to the privileged cant of upperclassmen on the basis of a single term?

"Where my father has decided, a 'word' is hardly sufficient to change his mind; you should know that!" Darcy replied tersely. "St. Jude's cannot be so bad if he choose it for you. What happened that you so wish to leave?"

George scowled in displeasure at his answer and deeper at his query. "Nothing happened! It is as I've said!" He made to get up, but then sat back down and leaned over the table toward Darcy, his face a picture of aggrieved injury. "Look, it's a runty little parson's son. Claims I took his precious compass. Well, he's a liar, the poxy cry baby," he looked over his shoulder, then back at Darcy and whispered, "but some of the lads have taken his part."

"Buy him a new one; they can't be more than a few shillings."

"Easy to say when you're 'Master Darcy,'" George sneered.

"It's better than a drubbing—"

"But impossible when there's no coin," George interrupted. "Spent it all," he added in response to Darcy's cocked brow. "One must make friends."

"Ask your father." The look George returned him clearly indicated his opinion of that recourse. "What will you do next term with no money?" Darcy asked in a lowered voice. "The purse my father gave you was meant to last the year. He will not replace it, I promise you, any more than he will send you to another school."

George shrugged his shoulders and looked down at the table. "You could lend me the money."

"Lend?"

"Well…give." George's face came up, a cunning light in his eyes. "It's no secret that I'm at St. Jude's on the Darcy shilling. Think of the scandal if I don't make things right with them at school! Hush it up and the Darcy name won't be tainted in any way."

Darcy frowned at him, not sure what to believe. He was not such a fool that he did not see the dangerous path George was inviting him to tread, but the threat of scandal had some merit. Should Father, stricken with grief as he was—as they all were—have to deal with scandal as well?

"All I need is a new start with the lads at school. Won't happen again, I swear." Contrition, like other useful emotions, sat easily upon George's face. Darcy pursed his lips. "Darcy, they'll throw me out! You know I must get on at school, or I'll end up no better than my father or worse!"

"Done!" Darcy bit out the word in exasperation. It was true. George would be dismissed in disgrace, and then what school would have him? It was also true that George might play this game again and again if he were not provided sufficient reason to curb his waywardness. "I'll give you what I can, but only this one time. You'll have to do be–"

"Of course, old man!" George drawled. "Straight and narrow from now on."

There it was again, that smug, maddening tone that made him burn to plant George a facer. Gripping the table's edge, Darcy gritted his teeth and shot to his feet. The kitchen fell silent at his sudden movement and looked from him to Wickham and back.

"What?" George looked up at him warily. "I *do* promise...word on it!"

His face hot from the sudden surge of anger, Darcy spit out, "See that you do, then, for it is the last!" and, turning his back on him, he strode out the kitchen door.

Chapter 4

Anger propelled Darcy up the three flights from the kitchen and down the hall to his old nursery. Slamming the door behind him, he collapsed against it, arms folded, and looked sharply about the room for anything that might distract him, anything that would absorb the crackling indignation that coursed through his body. Nothing suitable caught his eye. So, with a heart whose beat was even now beginning to calm, he pushed away from the door and set about regaining his composure with an inventory of the nursery's contents, shifting through it for those bits which might still be of interest to his cousins during their stay at Pemberley.

Richard was only a year older than himself, but D'Arcy was yet two more and would be entering University later next autumn. Perhaps, Darcy considered, his older cousin would wish to attach himself to the adults this year, rather than muck about with those he might regard now as mere boys. It was hard to tell with D'Arcy.

He spent the next two hours pulling out those games and model cannons, soldiers, and horses that might lend themselves to amusement and hiding away those toys from childhood that would excite an amusement of a different, disagreeable sort. When he had finished, the nursery had taken on the look of a young man's habitation rather than a child's and lacked only an appropriately sized table and set of chairs. He would mention that to Mrs. Reynolds after breakfast.

Satisfied with his labours, Darcy sped down the stairs to the breakfast room, his earlier meal in the kitchen quite a thing of the past. The serving dishes were at the ready on the sideboard, steam rising and condensing on their silver lids. Darcy looked at the table. Only two settings. Mother would not be coming down. His stomach clenched in apprehension as he sat. Was there more to what he had heard earlier this morning? There was no one he could ask, no one who would tell him the whole truth except, perhaps, his father. And yet, did he really wish to know?

The door opened, and a kitchen maid entered and curtsied upon seeing him. "Excuse me, Master Darcy, but Cook wants the dishes back to the kitchen. The master willna' be down for another half an hour or more. Will you be eating now, sir, or waiting for the master?"

"I'll wait for...no, I'll eat now, Betsy," he replied. Suddenly, he had his answer; he didn't want to know, could no longer stand the hush, the confused and worried tentativeness of everyone around him. He would take some breakfast and then—do what? He looked out the window at the sparkling snow. He would go for as hard a ride as nature and his horse would allow!

Betsy nodded and, moving to the sideboard, lifted each lid as Darcy helped himself to oatmeal with sweet cream, sausage and mashed potatoes, kippers, and rolls with butter and more orange marmalade.

Before Betsy left with the dishes on a tray, he secured a cold veal pie for later.

It was only a moment after Betsy left that Reynolds, entered. Bowing, he enquired, "Is everything as you wish, Master Darcy? The master will not be down for another hour and Cook wished to keep everything warm and fresh."

"Everything is very well, Reynolds. I had thought to wait," he added, "but..." *But what?* Although Reynolds was a trusted family retainer, he did not owe him an explanation, especially when he had none to give! He changed his tone. "Please send down to the stable that I desire Trojan to be ready in the courtyard within the hour and that I require no one to accompany me."

"Very good, Master Darcy," Reynolds bowed again, "and where shall I inform the master you have gone and when you mean to return?"

Here was a stumper! But Darcy was fixed and not to be deterred. "I'm going riding...to Lambton. I'll return by two."

"Very good. Some hot water soon upon your return, perhaps?" Reynolds prompted.

"Yes, of course," Darcy assented, beginning to wonder exactly who was planning this escape.

"It shall be done. Will that be all, Master Darcy?"

"Yes...except," he hesitated under Reynolds's expectant eye. Then, with guilty swiftness, it came to him, and he plunged ahead. "Send my compliments to Her Ladyship and say that I shall wait upon her when I return."

"Yes, *very* good, sir," Reynolds regarded Darcy approvingly and bowed, leaving him to his breakfast and the confidence that he had both secured his own wishes and admirably performed his duty.

Finishing quickly, Darcy raced with care back to his room. It would not do to arouse the interest of anyone on the family's floor if he were to make a good escape. He gained his room, rifled through a closet and found his riding coat and an old great coat with a woollen muffler tucked in the sleeve. Gloves and a battered tricorne hat completed his gear. Divesting himself of his morning coat, he struggled into a riding coat that now seemed a bit tight in the shoulders and short in the sleeve and exchanged his shoes for riding boots. He added the great coat atop the other and dropped the veal pie, wrapped in a napkin, in one of the large pockets. He scooped the remaining clothing up for a surreptitious return to the main floor and out to the courtyard.

The air was sharp with cold when Darcy stepped out onto the stairs leading down to the courtyard and the mounting block. He wrapped the muffler around his neck and brought an edge up over his chin and mouth. A shivering stable lad, dressed in a fantastical mis-match of clothing against the cold, held Trojan ready at the block, and Darcy hurried down the stairs.

"Toby," Darcy acknowledged the boy with a nod of appreciation.

"M-morning, Master Darcy," the lad returned politely, then added, "It be a chill ride today, but Trojan is that ready to be off. He may be a handful."

Darcy smiled behind his muffler as he ran a rough, gloved hand roughly over Trojan's neck. The horse tossed his head, letting out a stream of warm, foggy breath before nickering his second to Toby's warning. Darcy laughed. "Then we'd best get to it!" Toby bent and cupped his hand to give him a leg up, and he was soon secure in the stirrups and gathering the reins. "I'm off then," he nodded to Toby. "Back by two."

"Yes, Master Darcy." the boy tugged at his forelock and then scurried back to the warmth of the stable.

The clatter of Trojan's hooves on the courtyard gave way to muffled thumps on the snow-laden drive. The beast was as ready for excitement as Toby had said, pushing his gait into a stiff-legged trot that let Darcy know he was impatient to stretch into a faster one. His master was all too ready to oblige, but not quite yet. Wisdom cautioned that they should re-acquaint themselves after a term away from summer's frequent adventures. Regardless, Trojan tossed his head and pushed against the restraint of bridle and bit for half the length of Pemberley's long drive before settling down to a less jarring gait.

As they came to a stop at the tall iron gates that guarded the entrance to Pemberley, the gatekeeper, still struggling into his coat, popped out of his house and hurried over to open them. "No one sent word, Master Darcy!" he exclaimed with a tug at his hat and a worried look. "An' I didna' hear you comin' in all this snow!" He turned then to his task while Trojan stamped a hoof and snorted with impatience at the delay.

"Manners, Trojan!" Darcy scolded and then assured the man as he pulled open the ponderous sentinels, "Be easy; I sent no word, Jacob. Back by two," he warned. Nodding his thanks, he and Trojan left behind his ancestral lands with the express intention of escaping for a few hours the wrenching grip of sorrow and fear that had taken possession of it.

Once on the road to Lambton, Darcy loosed his restraint and allowed both Trojan and himself the release of a good run. The horse's hooves kicked up an appalling amount of slush and mud, spattering him from head to toe, but what did it matter? The sense of abandon, of freedom was exactly what he needed! The cold air set his lungs to burning and his eyes to watering, but it felt marvellous, it felt…alive!

It was not long before the smoke of hearth fires from the habitations on the outskirts of Lambton came into view. Darcy pulled back slightly on the reins, urging his mount to slow to a walk, and then finally, to stop. He observed the rising smoke uneasily. Reluctant to enter the village quite yet, he considered his options. Ahead, he knew, lay a path that veered off through some woods to a collection of outlying farms. Eventually, it wound its way back to Lambton from the other side, but it would afford him another hour of solitude if he kept Trojan in check. Darcy signalled Trojan onto the path that avoided the village. *Freedom and adventure!* He laughed at himself. *Well, freedom anyway.*

They passed through the wood at a fast walk, Trojan's ears twitching and head swinging from side to side, alert to any excuse for a display of startled surprise as they made their way. Darcy settled down in the saddle and enjoyed the stark beauty of the snow-laden wood and the warmth emanating from his companion's powerful body. Unfortunately, that warmth did not extend to his booted feet. They were beginning to send warnings. He would have to do something about that but hoped that he could put it off until he reached Lambton. *In for a penny, in for a pound,* he thought ruefully and wondered how far it would be before the village came back into sight.

They broke through the wood into open snow-swept fields. The cold intensified. Wind that had only stirred the upper branches of the trees in the wood now blew with unimpeded strength across the fields. Trojan arched his back like a cat and shivered from head to tail. Darcy wrapped his muffler around his mouth and nose again. *Oh, but it was wicked cold!*

His eyes narrowed against the stinging wind, Darcy peered ahead. There should be an old barn or stock house of some sort along this path if he remembered correctly. Closer to the next copse of trees, perhaps. He urged Trojan on, tears from the wind's assault blurring his vision. Yes, there it was! A dark shape formed against the copse, grew slowly larger and then resolved into a structure so decrepit he almost despaired of finding a serviceable entrance. Trojan needed no encouragement. He turned to the barn's shelter and trotted around it, seeking respite on the leeward side where he stopped and turned his head, inquiring of Darcy with his great brown eye what he next meant to do. Darcy dropped the reins, kicked his boots out of the stirrups, and was just about to throw his leg over when a loud *thwack* followed by a crowing shout startled both of them. He stiffened and froze, then scrambled for the reins as Trojan danced away in fright, nearly dumping him unceremoniously upon the snowy barnyard. Once more in control, he slid off and cautiously led the horse back and tied him up to the first post that gave some promise of tethering him against another fright.

"Shush," he crooned lowly and stroked the nervous beast's neck when another *thwack* and then another echoed from inside the barn, this time followed by laughter. "I'll be right back. Promise!" With a last reassuring stroke, he slipped away to find some way into the barn.

It didn't take long to find an entrance; the path through the snow that hedged the barn beaten by whoever was inside was easily discernable. It led to a dark, ragged gap in the tall wooden door that looked just large enough for him to squeeze through into the barn's musty protection. Removing his tricorne, he bent to the gap and listened.

"Start again, you blockhead, and this time remember: 'flies' not 'fleas!' It's got to rhyme."

"I know, I know." A second boy answered the first. "But just you 'ware of that there sword and mind the steps."

Swords and rhymes? Dumbfounded, Darcy leaned in through the gap and struggled through to the inside. Mounds of old straw lay heaped in shadows, but further in, the light of a lantern illuminated the centre of the barn floor. He stopped where he was for a moment, blinking, the darkness swirling around him until his snow blindness receded. As he waited a third voice, high and clear, began to intone.

What ho! What ho! Make room for mummers,
And old Anna Domino.
I have brought my champions brave,
Fighting men and Pedlar knave,
Old Doctor Spinny sometimes called Quack,
His man Salt Peter and old Fat Jack.
Old Father Christmas, so old and white,
He has promised to look in tonight.

Mummers! Darcy frowned in surprise. Mummers, local villagers who got up Christmas plays, were always men, but that voice surely belonged to a girl, and the others were just boys. *What was this!* Staying down, he made his way toward the light and the cleared area in the middle of the barn. The shadows of the young players jumped and skipped upon the walls as he crawled as close as he dared over the straw and surveyed the scene.

Four boys and the girl he'd heard stood shivering and hopping from foot to foot around a lantern and a jumble of what Darcy took to be their meagre supply of costume and props. Two of the boys stepped away, swinging crude wooden swords, and faced an imaginary audience.

Here come I the Royal Duke of Blunderland,
With my Broad Sword all in my hand,
Where is the man that dares bid me stand,
I'll slay him and cut him as small as Fleas–"

The other members of the little troupe groaned. One of them threw a clump of something at him, hitting him squarely on the back.

"Flies," cried the boy, "Flies!"

 −cut him as small as *Flies,*
 And send him to the Cookshop to make Mince-
    pies.
 Mincepies hot or mincepies cold,
 I'll send him to the Devil before he's three days
    old−

The other boy took a step beyond his fellow and with a deadly serious face declaimed his lines to the imaginary spectators.

 I am the man that dares to bid you stand,
 'Altho' you swaggers and swears that with your
    courageous hand,
 You will slay me and cut me as small as Flies,
 And send me to the Cookshop to make Mince-
    pies,
 Defend yourself for I show no Mercy,
 I fight to the death as sure as I am Earl Percy.

With that, the two squared off and with great cries sprang to the attack, producing a good deal of *thwacking* with the clumsy wooden swords as well as *thumps* when a blow landed on a backside or shoulder. Darcy was sorely tempted to laugh. The village lads hadn't the first idea of proper form or delivery, so the fight was little more than a close-quartered beating, the "swords" wielded more like cudgels. Finally the one designated to defeat clutched his side, let out a shriek and stumbled about the area with enthusiasm before finally falling to the ground.

The third boy then came forward and cried,

> Call the doctor, call old Quack,
> Take my donkey to bring him back.

A knock sounded and the girl hopped forward, a huge fake nose tied to her head.

"Come in Doctor Quack," the boy bowed.

With a puffed chest and stiff walk, the girl stalked back and forth, delivering her lines with a deep voice,

> I am not a Quack, as you may see,
> I am Doctor Spinney with a big M. D.
> I am a Doctor, a Doctor Good,
> Who's hand were stained with blood,
> I can cure the Pox, the Palsy, and the Gout,
> Pains within and pains without,
> If the Devil's in, I can fetch him out.

Darcy smiled. She was quite good actually. The nose and stance made her ridiculous, as was called for by the part, but she knew her lines and her character. A village girl, no less! *How unusual!*

> I have Plaster and Potions, Poisons and Pills,
> Some to cure and some to kill,
> I have travelled thro' England, Ireland, France and
>   Spain,
> Been to Europe and back again,
> Hocus, Pocus, Alecampain,

Take one of my Pills, Dead Man, rise and fight
   again–

She made a grand gesture to the audience, holding a large pill between her fingers, before stooping and placing the pill in the mouth of the deceased swordfighter.

This set the dead Duke to twitching and jerking and making the most amazing faces as he came back to life. Darcy chuckled and then, finally, unable to quell it, he laughed aloud.

"What was that?" one of the boys hissed and all the players froze where they were. Darcy clamped a hand over his mouth and lay quiet in the straw. *Four lads*, he quickly calculated the odds. He might be in for it. The silence was shattered by a snort and jangle of his bridle as Trojan shook himself outside.

"A horse!" the girl exclaimed. "Someone's here!"

"Find um!" ordered the Earl. "Stinkin' spies!" The other lads started forward, fanning out in search for him.

The cat's out of the bag now, Darcy grimaced. Better to make a stand than be dragged from the straw like a thief. Carefully, he rose from his hiding place, firmly planting his feet, his hands up and forming into ready fists to give as well as he was given.

The boys' eyes must have been too accustomed to the lantern light, for it took them a few seconds to discover him as he stood silent and, he hoped, looking confident. That much he had learned in his term at Eton; that much and maybe just enough more to come out of this with a whole skin.

"Hey, there 'e is!" the Duke cried.

It was time to take the lead. Darcy gave them all a chance to locate him and then strode purposefully forward into the circle of lantern light.

The troupe quickly gathered around him, although Darcy moved to keep any of them from his back. They were a mixed lot in age. Most of them near to him, including the girl, but two looked to be closer to fifteen or sixteen. What they all had in common was hostility, but even now some uncertainty was creeping into their faces. They obviously had no idea who he was.

"Hey now," the biggest lad said with menace, "just who are you?" He tapped one of the wooden swords against his thigh. "I ain' never seen you a'fore."

One of the other lads then piped up, "You're from Klypton, come to spy on us, you are, no mistake!" That seemed to inspire general agreement among the troupe. A spy from Klympton sounded dangerous enough, but it did offer Darcy a way of avoiding the first question, which he found himself reluctant to answer. The truth would put a period to this adventure he had stumbled upon. It would also end, abruptly and badly, if he did not put on a bold front.

Imitating old Samuel Coachman's Derbyshire drawl, he bellowed out a derisive laugh, "Klympton! Theys couldna get a line right to save their ruddy souls! You lads have already got 'em beat!" It was, admittedly, a shot in the dark but it immediately found a mark.

"S'truth?" asked the other lad with a sword. "We were that worried with Rosie here—"

"Rosamund!" the girl corrected in a voice long with irritation. Her eyes were wide in curious examination of him. Keeping in character, he boldly returned her regard, but in that moment experienced a strange, and not unpleasant, tingle go up his spine. *What is this?* He transferred his gaze back to the other lads.

"Yes, s'truth!" he asserted to grins breaking out all around. "But they do have one thing on you."

"Yeah, theys not got to 'ave a girl in the—ouch!" The lad next to Rosamund started hopping about on one foot and holding the other. "Rosie!"

"Rosamund!" she repeated firmly and this time smiled quite a pretty smile at Darcy. "What 'ave they got?"

That strange feeling trilled through him again, but he pushed on. He had their full attention, even if it was not entirely friendly.

"They-uns know sword-play. You lads, well...you lads are rough." He shook his head as if the words pained him.

"We jus' gotta practice more, an' we'll do," the Earl claimed, waving his hand. "We will!" he repeated to a growing chorus of groans. He turned on Darcy. "An' who are you, anywise?"

"Will."

The name slipped out of Darcy's mouth before he'd even thought. It was common enough and close enough that he wouldn't forget who he was supposed to be. It would do, and suddenly he wanted it to more than "do." He crossed his arms over his chest and looked the "Earl" straight in the eyes.

"An' I'm the lad what can show you how to make the sword-play look true."

Chapter 5

A general uproar greeted Darcy's claim, most of the boys pressing toward him with eager faces, but the "Earl" stood his ground. " 'ere now!," he growled, his arms wide against the others attempting to surge past him, "I'm the captain o' this company, and I say, afore you bring out the welcome cup, he should prove his fine words."

With all eyes upon him, Darcy nodded. It was no less than he expected. Lads were lads, whether on the playing fields of Eton or the barnyards of Lambton. He swept his tricorne off his head and started on the buttons of his great coat as the troupe stepped back to give them room and the "Earl," who topped him by at least four inches, smiled down at him with the bravado of one accustomed to command. He shucked off the old great coat and kicked it aside. The coat had suffered from the muck of the road, but his riding jacket beneath, though markedly too small for him, was in good order. Some sharp whistles told him that its quality had not escaped notice. Quickly, he drew it off and threw it down with the rest, then stepped up to his adversary, drawing attention back to the excitement of the challenge that had been issued.

"If sum'un will lend me a poker, lessons can start!" Barks of laughter from Darcy's audience encouraged him to think that the clothes were forgotten. The contest was all.

"Here!" The Duke tossed him his crudely carved sword. "An' give him summat he give me, iffn' yer able." He postured broadly and rubbed his backside to further laughter.

Darcy grinned at the comedy and nodded, but his attention was centred on his opponent. The youth had no knowledge of swordsmanship, but his height and weight would give him considerable advantage if this demonstration turned into a brawl. "Yer name?" he asked him as space was made for the contestants.

"Jack," the "Earl" replied, his manner grown serious. He gripped his sword's pommel tightly and brought it up to an awkward approximation of an *en guard* position.

"Your feet are all wrong," Darcy advised him with a grimace and then shook his head, "and you're too extended. Pull in your elbow...like this." He demonstrated the proper stance.

"I ain' takin' a lesson," Jack growled. "It's you who's provin' his salt." He hardened his stance and addressed the "Duke," though his stare remained centred on Darcy. "Well, Rob, are ya goin' ta say the word to start this jig, or are we—"

"On wif it!" Rob yelled, and the rest took up the cry. Some encouraged Jack to "show 'em" and others urged "Will" to do the same and "be smart about it." Darcy let his opponent come at him, parrying his undisciplined charge. It was as he had guessed; Jack had no form or discipline, wielding his erstwhile sword as little more than a bludgeon. As a bludgeon, however, it was quite effective. Darcy's fingers and wrist rang numbly already from the force of Jack's assault. Disappointed hoots and jeers rose from the audience.

"Come on, show summat!"

"At him, Jack! There's a stroke!"

A cheer went up as Darcy staggered under another blow upon his sword. A broad grin replaced the narrow ferocity on Jack's face. Darcy's guess that Jack would test his success with another of the same proved true. This time, instead of meeting the blow, he stepped back and in one fluid movement dropped, rolled backward and regained his stance, leaving Jack to beat thin air. The troupe howled with delight.

Satisfied that he now knew his opponent, Darcy began his offensive. His next parry did more than merely deflect but sent his opponent sideways. He followed it quickly with the flat of the "sword" on Jack's backside. The resulting thwack and surprised grunt from his adversary were highly gratifying and not unappreciated by his audience. He then enlarged upon that surprise with a forward advance and feint, causing Jack to jump backward in an awkward attempt to protect himself from a blow that never came. Laughter from their audience, however, did; and the effect was instantaneous. Red-faced, Jack roared and made to charge back, but Darcy had advanced upon him. It was all he could do to defend against the darting tip of Darcy's sword as he teased him with thrusts to the left, then the right, high, then low.

Exultation coursed through Darcy as he pressed his advantage. The temptation to thoroughly route his opponent followed hard upon it. Jack's face signalled his exasperation and the dawning fear of an humiliated defeat. Was that what he wanted—to shame Jack in front of his comrades? Darcy dropped his arm slightly, his indecision informing his body rather than the discipline of swordplay. With the quick reflexes of the cunning, Jack recognised an opening and rose up over Darcy with a guttural cry, his sword high and held with both hands. If he succeeded in delivering that blow, Darcy knew it would break his collarbone or his wrist if he tried to parry it. His only hope lay in the unexpected. Swiftly, he darted forward. A look of surprise passed quickly over his adversary's face just before Darcy delivered a hard jab to Jack's ribs and slipped under and around him. Jack doubled over, and the sword completed its terrible descent to the floor, the crack echoing throughout the barn as it splintered.

"Awwww!" groaned Jack, dropping to his knees, his arms wrapped around his middle. The troupe gasped and then looked at them both in silence. Darcy's smile of victory faded. His jab at Jack had been only enough to set him on his heels, nothing more. Did they think otherwise? Would they congratulate him on a good show or turn on him now that he had bested their chief? He looked down at his adversary and knew he had to make him an ally and quickly!

With a flick of his wrist, Darcy sent the wooden sword into a mound of straw and stepped up to Jack, hand outstretched. "Here," he offered, "you were splendid...truly! Cry friends, Jack?"

"Uh-ah!" Jack's head came up, a fierce scowl distorting his face, but it could be just from the pain. Perhaps he'd jabbed him harder than he'd thought. "Uh-ah!" he bellowed again as he brought one knee up and began slowly to straighten to a stand.

"Ya alright there, Jack?" Rob asked, still a safe distance away.

"Right...ah...right as rain, Robbie," Jack groaned but continued to rise. "Nothin's broke. S'far as I can tell he jist poked ma breadbox a good'un. Which," he continued, turning his attention to Darcy, "is a bit less 'an I had planned for 'im." He eyed Darcy's proffered hand. "Friends is it? Ya know I was that angered I'd 'ave broken yer shoulder?"

Darcy nodded. "I know, and my hand's still out." He returned Jack's scrutiny with a steady gaze while the others shifted uneasily.

"Oh!" Her voice rising in exasperation, Rosamund broke from the group and skipped over to them. "Take his hand, Jack!" she cajoled him. "Fair is fair, ya great lummox! An' think what a show we'll 'ave!" She looked at Darcy, her smile full and undisguised spreading up and into her eyes. Her face was so lively and her confidence so quickly given, shining there in her large dark eyes, that Darcy was speechless with pleasure despite the return of that unidentifiable frisson to plague his stomach and skip up and down his spine. She laughed. He smiled, sheepishly at first, and then with growing assurance as she took his arm and turned him to face the others. "Well then," she called to the rest, "who's first for lessons?"

~ ~ ~ ~ ~ ~ ~&~ ~ ~ ~ ~ ~ ~

Trojan was glad to see Darcy emerge from the old barn. The horse set out for home with a determination that would not be crossed. The wind continued cold as they travelled back to Pemberley, but Darcy hardly noticed until he was within sight of its gates. Warmed by his success at winning a place among the village lads and the unexpected pleasure he'd felt at schooling them in their sword-play, he spent the greater part of his journey wondering at the strange feelings that the girl, Rosamund, had sent ranging through him. He didn't know what was making him feel all at sixes and sevens. All he could determine was that the flash of intelligence and wit in her dark eyes was wonderful to contemplate.

Relinquishing Trojan's reins to the stable lad, he trotted off to the house. Mr. Reynolds, faithful to his word, had his bath ready in a trice and within an hour he was dressed and brushed, his hair smoothed back and tied into a neat queue, and pronounced ready to wait upon his mother. Standing there before her door, a queer sensation of dread and guilt at his own animal health worked upon him so that to lift his knuckles to rap upon the door seemed an unthinkable insult. *If he could only escape this duty!* Immediately, he was ashamed of himself. *Duty? He loved his mother, admired her above everything! What was wrong with him.* The door opened.

"Fitzwilliam?" Lady Anne stood in the doorway, her hand upon the knob. She smiled at the sight of him and stepped back.

"I thought I heard your footsteps in the hall. Please, come in, my dear. As you can see," she said, holding out her hand, "everything is prepared." Darcy stepped forward and with a hesitant smile took her hand.

"There now, come and see. I declare, it is a tea to end all teas! And so I told Reynolds." Lady Anne drew him into her side and gently propelled him to a low table in her sitting room that fairly groaned with every imaginable delicacy, all surmounted by a gleaming silver teapot.

"I heard you were out riding for hours, so you must be uncommonly hungry."

It was true; although he had not known it until that moment. *Bravo, Mrs. Reynolds!* he thanked her silently. "Yes, ma'm," he replied as he looked up at his mother, "quite hungry!"

Lady Anne laughed and hugged him briefly before releasing him and taking her seat. Darcy took the chair opposite and availed himself of a plate of the many tempting bits on display before him.

"Your tea, Fitzwilliam?" Darcy looked up to see Lady Anne holding out his dish of tea. Her arm trembled and some tea splashed over and into the saucer. "Oh!" she exclaimed as he hastened to take it from her. "Pardon my…my clumsiness. How stupid of me!"

"Mother, please," Darcy protested quietly. "Do not say so! You are only tired."

"Well, perhaps." She took up her own tea and relaxed back into her chair with a rueful smile. "I doubt that I was ever *very* clumsy."

Nor stupid, he thought. He sipped at the hot tea before chancing an upward glance. Despite the lines of pain that were beginning to etch her face and the new frailty he sensed about her, she remained a beautiful woman. She had acceded nothing to her illness, but had dressed in a fashionable gown with her hair dressed charmingly under a gauzy lace cap just to take tea with him.

"You must know that your Uncle and Aunt Matlock will arrive with your cousins at the end of the week," Lady Anne began. "Have you considered how you will prepare for their visit?"

His cousins! Darcy almost choked on his scone. How would he ever be able to continue with the mummer's play with his sharp-eyed cousins about, especially Richard, whose nose for a lark was unerring! The answer to that would have to wait, but he was in an excellent position to reassure his mother.

"Yes, ma'm," he was glad to reply. "I have put away the childish things from the nursery and arranged it more suitably for grown lads." He went on to describe the changes he had already made and his plans for entertaining his cousins.

"Well done!" The approval in her eyes warmed him. "You may also wish to consult your father. I believe he has a box or more of 'suitable' things for grown lads to contribute to your guests' entertainment."

Darcy brightened at that. *What might his father have tucked away?*

"I will, ma'm!"

His mother nodded and brought the delicate china cup to her lips but took only the smallest of sips before returning it to the saucer and both to the table. It was then that Darcy realized that she had not partaken of anything. She was not as well as she pretended. A coldness moved through him that made him shiver.

"As you know, it is my deepest wish, Fitzwilliam, that this Christmas be celebrated as we have always done." Lady Anne regarded him closely. "I have expressed this wish to your father as well. Everything must be done to ensure the comfort and happiness of our guests and in celebration of the season. I tell you this because more will fall to you than you may have expected." She closed her eyes, a brief sigh escaping her lips. Alarmed, Darcy rose, but she motioned him back.

"No, please, I am well enough." Her hands fluttered to her stomach and then down to smooth out her skirts. "The truth is that I may not be able to do as much…take part in as much as I have in the past. I tire so quickly now." Her voice trailed off.

"Mama?" Darcy exclaimed and moved to the edge of his chair, his fear growing. Should he call her maid?

"So," she took a shallow breath and began again, "you must be my lieutenant and help your father uphold the Pemberley traditions in my place. Can you do that, Fitzwilliam?"

"Yes, ma'm," Darcy whispered his promise.

"I know you will, my own, and do it well." Lady Anne sank further into her chair. "Ah, Fitzwilliam, I confess that it is you that I think about the most when I consider what lies ahead. Your dear father has dealt with this illness as well as I could hope...better, really. But we must speak of this, you and I." She closed her eyes and was silent long enough for Darcy to think she might have fallen asleep. But she stirred and he knew that she was only gathering strength to speak again.

"We must speak of the future now, as I am able, so you will know my heart, my best hopes for all of you. Alas, my child, little Georgiana...she will never know her mother, nor hear from my own lips my hopes for her. She is too young to know what you and your father feel. For that I am both grieved and grateful." She heaved a heavy sigh. "But you, Fitzwilliam, are at an awkward age. No longer a child and not yet a man. It is you I will regret leaving above all."

A sob threatened to escape Darcy. He managed to control himself enough to whisper, "Mama, please!"

"Oh, my dear one, let me say this while I have the strength and will to say it." She looked at him full on and took his hand in hers. "What I regret above all is that I will not see the man...the good man you will become."

Darcy's lungs heaved, desperate to relieve the tightness that gripped them. "Mama, do not say...I cannot..." He ducked his head and gulped. The tears he'd denied and the awful anguish threatened to tear him apart. "Mama!" he cried and, falling to his knees at her side, he laid his head in her lap and sobbed. Long shuttering sobs of utter despair racked his young frame. He clutched her skirts and gave himself up it.

Her fingers, soft and cool, stroked his hair. "There now," she whispered, "there now. 'Weeping may endure for a night,' Fitzwilliam. Do not neglect to look for the 'joy that cometh in the morning.' Is that not the promise of Christmas? We shall be together again at last! And from this day until then and forever, I shall always love you."

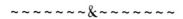

How long he lay with his head in her lap he didn't know. At some point, he knew he was empty of tears and grief. His mother's hands lay motionless on his head and he was brought to the present with a start of concern.

Lady Anne sat in an exhausted sleep. Darcy extracted himself from her delicate hold and went to find her maid. Together, they moved her to the comfort of her bed.

"You leave her to me now, Master Darcy," Miss Barrows said. "I know how to care for her when she's in this state. I have done it many a time this last week. She just needs her rest."

Darcy took a long look at his mother as she lay on her bed in the beautiful, formal dress she'd donned for his visit. Then, quietly, he walked down the hall to his own room.

The cold of another December day continued to hold the Derbyshire countryside in thrall as Darcy and Trojan descended the long winding drive to the great house at Pemberley. Darcy's days during this week before Christmas had fallen into a pattern: breakfast alone, a visit with Reynolds to see if there were instructions from his father or tasks his father required him to perform, a ride to the mummer's barn near Lambton for practice with the troupe, and a private visit with his mother in mid-afternoon when she was able. So preoccupied were his parents with her illness that he seldom saw either in the morning, though they managed dinner as a family most evenings.

So, it was not surprising that Darcy looked forward to the escape to Lambton each morning. He and Trojan both enjoyed the long rides, and Darcy was regaining fine riding trim after the time away at school. The mummer's practices were a welcome diversion from the troubles at home and had made the days pass quickly. It was now Thursday. Tomorrow, his cousins would arrive and he would have diversions of another sort.

The light dusting of new snow danced away from Trojan's hooves on their approach to the stable doors. Toby's head emerged as Darcy dismounted, stamping his feet to return circulation to his toes as he held out the reins to the stable lad.

"I've worked him hard, Toby. He'll need a good rub down before feeding, no matter what he tells you otherwise." Darcy ran a gloved hand over the beast's shoulder and patted it heartily.

"Yer rides 'ave been good for 'im, Master Darcy. He's lookin' fit an' has narry been up to so little mischief."

Bored with the conversation, Trojan snorted and nudged Toby toward the warmth of the stable.

"We're goin', Yer Highness, we're goin'! Master Darcy?" Toby tugged at his cap and, receiving his dismissal, turned to lead the horse to his comfortable box.

Darcy ascended the steps of the great house. Once inside, he discovered Pemberley's housekeeper awaiting him.

"Mrs. Reynolds!" He acknowledged her welcoming smile with a grin as he shrugged off his coat. "Does Father want me?"

"No, Master Darcy," she said and curtsied. Her smile broadened with the message she delivered. "Her Ladyship is feeling particularly well today and wishes for you to take tea with her this afternoon in Eden."

Darcy's face lit up. Eden, the conservatory, was his mother's most beloved corner of Pemberley. There, under her personal care and supervision, she had created such an extraordinary retreat of beauty and fruitfulness that her husband had declared it an "Eden," which, thenceforth, it remained in the parlance of the entire household. That Lady Anne felt strong enough to visit Eden was great news, indeed.

Thanking Mrs. Reynolds, Darcy raced up the stairs and to his bedchamber where no less a personage than the footman in training to his father's valet had everything in readiness, including a ewer of hot water for the basin. Little more than three quarters of an hour later, his hair brushed and retied and dressed in clean stockings and his second best coat and breeches for afternoon visits, he was declared fit to present himself to his mother.

Darcy pulled at his cuffs and smoothed his coat as he approached the doors to the conservatory. Was his mother's condition truly as improved as Mrs. Reynolds had indicated, or was it by force of will alone that she entertained him in Eden today rather than in her sitting room? A servant opened one of the doors, and with a determined intake of breath, Darcy decided to believe the former.

He found his mother seated at a table among the greenery, the bright December sun warm through the glass plates. The air was moist with the smell of earth, the fragrances of growing things and, as he drew nearer, the scent of tea, warm bread, and a delightful array of sweets.

"Fitzwilliam," his mother greeted him, "you are just returned from your daily ride."

"Yes, Mama." He bent and kissed her cheek before sitting opposite her. She did seem better. There was more colour in her face than he had seen since he'd come home.

"Tell me," she cajoled. "You have become quite the devoted horseman and in such weather!"

He described to her the beauties of the wintry countryside and the understanding growing between Trojan and him, of temperaments and tricks and contests of will. He did not, of course, speak of the mummers or even the barn where they met, although he suddenly wished that he could. Would she enjoy a recounting of his first meeting with them and laugh with him over his efforts to teach them a bit of swordplay? He considered her as he bit into a piece of buttered bread. No, he decided. His mother's laughter came easily and she, unlike his father, was always ready to place the best construction on anything he did. Even so, he could not chance such a thing.

"It is wonderful to see you here among your flowers again, ma'm," he declared, drawing the conversation away from more troublesome topics.

His mother looked appreciatively around her and spoke of what it meant to her to have this refuge of green in the Derbyshire winter. "It was your father's wedding gift to me, you know." Darcy nodded. The story was well known to him. "It was only glass and dirt and a few rare flowers clinging to life at the beginning, but it was rich with possibilities. Not unlike our marriage." She sipped her tea in silence, not looking at him but considering the lush colours of Eden's vegetation against the barrenness beyond the glass. He watched as she took a deep breath of the heavy air and slowly, slowly let it out. *Did she wait for him to say something?*

"Fitzwilliam, do you know how happy my marriage to your father has been?"

Darcy paused in mid-bite, startled by her question.

"We have been fortunate, happy beyond our hopes and far beyond the experience of many. Why do you think that is, my dear?" she queried him.

"I...I cannot guess, Mama!" he stuttered. "Because you are pretty and kind...and he is strong?"

She smiled at him but shook her head. "Have you thought of your own future life? How you will choose a wife, direct your children and your servants? What passions you will allow to command your time?"

He brightened. *There*, at last, was a question he could answer! "Father and Samuel Coachman have both promised to teach me to drive next summer! I want to become as good as Father was when he was a Four-and-Goer."

His response seemed to confound her, but in a few moments her puzzled expression melted into amusement. "Oh, Fitzwilliam!" she laughed. "That is exactly the answer I *should* have expected from a young man of thirteen." She replenished her tea cup and sipped some of the brew. Darcy could tell that she was thinking how to proceed and waited. She put down her cup and folded her hands in her lap.

"I see that the conversation I wished to have with you will not come as easily as I thought, and that I have been obscure where I had meant to be plain." She leaned forward and nudged a plate of biscuits toward him. He obliged her and piled several more on his plate.

"I suppose that it is horses and games and proving yourself that concerns you now, that is only natural. But it will not be very long before your thoughts will turn to female companionship and, eventually, to your responsibility to marry."

Responsibility? Darcy was once more surprised. He had never thought of marriage as a responsibility. It was just what one did when grown. As for the bit about "female" companionship... He blushed and moved uncomfortably in his chair. This *was* deep water!

"Your choice of wife will be the most important decision you ever make, Fitzwilliam," his mother continued. "It will, in large part, determine your own happiness and the success of Pemberley in the future. It is a decision you must not take lightly. It is a decision you must prepare for even now as a schoolboy at Eton." Lady Anne considered him for a moment before continuing.

"I know that marriage must seem a very dull topic to young man contemplating driving a team of horses, but I fear I may not have another opportunity before you are off again to school. I promise to keep my advice concise so that we may proceed to other subjects. Agreed?"

"Agreed, Mama," Darcy answered.

"Well, now, some requirements for your choice of wife. She must come from a good family, Fitzwilliam, the *best* family. This you must do for the honour and dignity of Pemberley." Lady Anne took a sip of tea.

"Secondly, she must be your social equal with manners that reflect well upon you in every situation—in Town or in the country. You must do this for your *own* sake. Your wife's manners—her speech, deportment, behaviour—cannot be an embarrassment to you, Fitzwilliam, or you will never respect her or know peace. Do you understand me?"

"I believe so, Mama. But..." Darcy spread his hands hopelessly. "I know nothing of girls. How am I to choose?"

His mother laughed again. "You mustn't worry about that now. It will all happen in good time. You will meet many girls in the years to come, Fitzwilliam. You will learn how they think and act, what attracts you and what does not. I dare say you will have many admirers since you are rich and grow more handsome by the day." Darcy blushed at his mother's enthusiasm.

"That is the danger, Fitzwilliam, for there will be many young ladies who will wish to become mistress of Pemberley." She leaned toward him and held out her hand. He took it, soft and light, in his. "I know you will be guided by your Father in this when the time is appropriate, but, for your happiness, choose a woman who is your equal in taste and feeling, a woman who respects and honours you and for whom you feel the same. If you remember and act on this advice, Fitzwilliam, you will be well and I can be content."

Chapter 6

D arcy watched as Farley stumbled into the lantern light in his role as the drunkard Fat Jack.

I am a button maker by my trade,
Till I was ruined by a Maid,
Damn such Maids, so said I,
Fall rall riddle roll a rye.

Farley played up his small part to the hilt, tripping and swaying in a wide circle with eyes crossed and his nose reddened with clay. Sitting beside Darcy, Rosamund alternately laughed and moaned as Fat Jack took every opportunity to embellish his role.

"Farley!" she cried. "Give over; yer actin' such a fool!" She leaned closer to Darcy and whispered, "Mum swears he must have fallin' on his head, he's such a one fer silliness. The school master won't have him but in the corner." Darcy laughed with her but that didn't prevent the shiver that Rosamund's intimate manner sent coursing through his body. For some inexplicable reason all he could think about was the dimple in her cheek when she smiled at him and the sudden, strong desire to touch her hair or take her hand that was playing havoc with his emotions.

Here come I old Fat Jack,
At fighting I can do my whack
By Day, or Night, or candlelight,

Old Jack will Fight, with all his might,
Wrong or right, sober or tight.

"Yah, tight it'll haf to be!" yelled Teague, the boy who
had the part of Salt Peter. "Old Jack" clumsily drew his
sword and brandished it in the direction opposite his heck-
ler. Laughing, Rosamund slipped away from her perch at
Darcy's side and took her place for the next part. Darcy
straightened and shifted his violin under his arm as he
watched her skip to her place, tossing a wink at him over
her shoulder.

She was entirely unlike any girl he had ever met. Truth
be told, he had never been on such easy terms with any
other. The girls of his limited experience were carefully
chaperoned and deadly dull. They seemed to do nothing
but practice their simpers with each other and regard young
gentlemen of his age as quite beneath their regard. Not so
with Rosamund. Her smile was quick and genuine; her eyes
brimmed with a native wit that just suited his temperament
and made him glad to be her confidante. This week of
stolen hours in her company and that of the other young
mummers had been jolly good fun even were it not for
those oft occurring warm impulses toward her that excited
and confused him.

None of them had questioned him further on his origins;
although they must know that he was not really one of
them. No matter that his carefully chosen clothes did not
bespeak "gentry," his horse could not help but place him
above their touch. But for the moment, they had accepted
him, taken his instruction in sword-play in good humour,
and rewarded his efforts with giving him a part in the play.

By this time, Old Fat Jack's peregrinations had come to
an end. Having walked blindly into a post, he was down on

the ground, a hand to his jaw. Rosamund, as Doctor Spinney, was upon him in a flash.

> He's got the Toothache.
> Why it is quite big,
> And will bring forth a New-Heir-Year,
> On the 31st of December at 12 p.m!
> Salt Peter fetch Pinchers; we will have a tooth out,
> And make sure, it will make the Bill longer!

Teague hurried forth flourishing a pair of tongs that, from the size of them, had last seen service in a horse's mouth. The "Doctor" snatched them away and with many grunts and twists accompanied by tremblings and screams from the sufferer, the "tooth" was pulled and the traditional "Pill" administered. Old Fat Jack jumped back to instantaneous full health. That was Darcy's cue. Knocking on the post he called out:

> Here come I, a Pedlar Chap,
> On my shoulder I car's my pack,
> I have ribbons for the Ladies fair,
> Ornaments to deck their Hair,
> Patches for their Pretty Faces,
> High-heeled Boots and fine Laces,
> Toys to please both great and small,
> And I've brought my Fiddle to please you all.

Darcy brought his violin up under his chin and played a tune to match the energy of the Morris dance which the troupe bravely executed with fewer missteps than earlier that week. As he played, their leader slipped out for a costume change, returning as Father Christmas with a flowing beard of sheep's wool. The performers danced him into their midst, and Darcy exchanged the dance tune for that of the final piece of their performance, a song sung out by the whole troupe:

> A virgin unspotted the Prophets foretold,
> Should bring forth a Saviour which we now be
>   hold,
> To be our redemption from Death, Hell and Sin,
> Which Adam's transgressions involved us in,
> So let us be merry; cast Sorrow away,
> Christ Jesus our Saviour was born on this day.

When the last note ended and "Earl" Jack had quickly whispered, "One, two, three," they all took their bows. "Well now," Jack said as he nodded at them all, pleasure evident in his voice, "that was well done, lads! Well done! We'll show those Klympton boys." He clapped Darcy on the back. "Won't we, Will?"

~ ~ ~ ~ ~ ~ ~ & ~ ~ ~ ~ ~ ~ ~

Darcy was about to mount Trojan when he felt a delicate tug on the sleeve of his greatcoat. He looked over his shoulder. It was Rosamund.

"Hey, Will." Her smile dissolved into a chattering of teeth in the cold, but her eyes were warmly bright and teased an answering smile from him.

"Yes?"

"Doan be f-forgettin', now! Sunday night, the s-square hard by the church on High Street."

Darcy swallowed uneasily. Christmas Eve…when he and his entire family would be attending services inside that self same church. How was he ever going to escape the congregation, perform with the mummers, and rejoin his family without notice? And what about his costume and violin?

"Will?" Rosamund prompted.

"I won't forget," he responded. "I'll be there!" Inwardly, Darcy groaned. Deeper and deeper! He really should get home before he promised anything more.

Rosamund's smile turned into a delighted laugh, and to Darcy's surprise, she reached out and stroked Trojan's neck. Ever hopeful, the horse craned about and lipped at the ends of her shawl as he searched for a treat.

"Trojan!" Darcy admonished him.

"That be his name? Trojan?"

Darcy nodded, suddenly glad for an excuse to linger in Rosamund's company.

"I love horses and he's a beautiful one! Are ya not, Trojan?" She patted the animal and glanced at Darcy. "An it's sure that you're a dashin' sight on him, Will."

The compliment caught him unprepared and so was he also for the quick squeeze that she gave his hand.

"There's a surprise I have for ya, Will," Rosamund whispered. "Sunday. After the play. Remember!"

~ ~ ~ ~ ~ ~ ~ & ~ ~ ~ ~ ~ ~ ~

He was late, and worse, in disgrace! He knew it from the look on every face from the gatekeeper's to Reynolds's, even to the kitchen boy who filled his bath. His uncle, aunt, and cousins were due to arrive at any moment and here he was, still in his room, racing to get dressed. How blithely he had squandered precious moments on those mummer lads!

Mummers! What were you thinking? he harshly reprimanded himself. He shoved his arms through the coat the footman held up for him and pulled the cuffs free before tugging at the whole to set the shoulders aright.

Here come I a Pedlar Chap,
On my shoulder I car's my pack…

Lines from the play flittered through his mind. However
unsound his adventure might seem now, it had been such
fun and the camaraderie so easy! He even had a part in it if
he dared take it. *Did he dare?* How could he manage it all,
especially when his cousins were here? He could hardly
imagine dodging Richard for any length of time. What
would be the troupe's chances if he let them down? Did he
not, as a gentleman, owe even them his word? And that
girl, Rosamund…what would she think of him?

The faint jingle of harness bells crept through his bedchamber window. They were come! Darcy ran to the window. Yes, indeed, it was his cousins! The Matlock travelling
coach appeared dark against the snow as the driver made
his final approach, its four horses brightly accented with
silver bells on every surface of harness and mistletoe and
holly twined in their carefully combed manes and tails. It
could have been the conveyance of Father Christmas himself! As the coach pulled past his window, one of its windows flew down and his cousin Richard's merry face appeared.

"Darcy!" he yelled, hanging out the window and then
sticking out his tongue before being whisked back inside by
a strong, gloved hand. Darcy laughed aloud and wheeled
toward the door. One could always depend upon Richard!

"Master Darcy!" the footman yelped. "Your hair, sir!"

"Hmm? Yes, of course." Darcy raced back to his dressing table and grabbed his brushes. Pushing his hair into a
semblance of order, he tied the ribbon fast round his queue

and ran out the door and down the hall, only to come upon his parents about to embark on their slow, careful descent of the stairs.

"Fitzwilliam!" his father cautioned sharply.

"Yes, sir," he said, skidding to a stop. "Your pardon, sir."

Lady Anne gave him a curious look. Too guilty to answer the question in her eyes, Darcy looked down at his feet. Father and Mother both passed him by and began their descent. Behind them followed Nurse with a ribbon-bedecked Georgiana on her hip.

"Fis!" she called softly and solemnly attempted to wink at him, but her cheeks would not cooperate and her attempt ended as a blink.

> *I have ribbons for the Ladies fair,*
> *Ornaments to deck their Hair…*

"Dolly!" Darcy whispered back to her and winked in response as Nurse carried her giggling down the stairs.

Below, the doors were already flung open and Lady Cecelia Matlock flowed through them in a haste born of the cold and a close familiarity. Darcy looked down over the banister to see his aunt, skirts and cape billowing, almost run into the hall.

"Darcy!" she exclaimed, shivering. "That wind! I thought we would be shaken to bits!"

"Cecelia," his father greeted his aunt with a broad smile and a kiss upon her reddened cheeks. "Welcome and come to the fire! Here," he continued, arresting her cold, gloved hands in their fruitless attempt to untie the ribbons of her bonnet, "allow me."

"Matlock," he nodded in greeting at his brother-in-law now entering the hall. "Happy Christmas!"

"And to you, Darcy!" Lord Matlock removed his hat and handed it to the footman. "More happy to be greeted by some of your Fire and Brimstone, though. Damned cold drive, I tell you, not to mention being boxed up with those hellions of mine." He shook his greatcoat from his shoulders and, after bestowing it also upon the waiting servant, turned to his sister.

"Anne!" he exclaimed in concern and embraced her. "My dear, should you be standing here in this cold?" He looked over at his brother-in-law. "Darcy, what do you mean by allowing—"

"Matlock, you know better than to cast me as the villain. Your sister would not be dissuaded—"

Shouts from outside the doors put a point to his protest and drew down Lord Matlock's brow in a most ominous manner. Darcy ran down the rest of the stairs as, with an awful grimace, Lord Matlock turned on his heel to confront the latest in a long string of his progeny's transgressions. "Boys!" he bellowed, "I will nail your—"

Swoosh! A snowball blazed through the hall and struck his uncle full upon the chest, then traced a wet trail down the front of his coat and breeches and landed upon the hall floor. Darcy bit down upon a laugh and stared as his two cousins, D'Arcy and Richard Fitzwilliam, peered carefully into the hall. For a moment, all was silent while a multitude of expressions played across Lord Matlock's face.

"Ah-ha!" A long, deep laugh broke from Darcy's father. "Matlock," he finally gasped, " the look …your face!" Uncle Matlock turned to his father, his brow raised askance at such disregard for his umbrage, but this sent not only Darcy's father, but his mother, also, into peals of laughter. Aunt Matlock began to giggle and soon, even his uncle was battling the rueful smile that tugged at his lips. Encouraged by the laughter, the brothers took small, hesitant steps just inside the doors, all the while maintaining a wary eye upon their father.

"D'Arcy...Richard! Come in before you freeze and your aunt catches cold," Darcy's father called. He motioned to a footman to remove the offending projectile. "What a splendid snowball and jolly well thrown! Though, perhaps not so well aimed?"

"No, sir," Richard squeaked immediately, grateful for the opening his uncle had provided. "Dodgy aim to be sure!"

~ ~ ~ ~ ~ ~ ~ & ~ ~ ~ ~ ~ ~ ~

"Fitz, tell me that you did not...please!" It was Friday night. Richard leaned across the table in the former nursery, the wreckage of battle lying in a mute tumble of toy soldiers, horse and cannon between them. Darcy grimaced and shrugged his shoulders. "Ahh, that my own cousin could be gulled so easily and by that little snake!" Richard collapsed back into his chair with a disgusted cry and shook his head. "I've failed, failed miserably, D'Arcy!"

"Well," drawled his brother, "you managed to get him through First Term with only a few bruises. There's something in that!" D'Arcy turned to his cousin. "But how you could allow Snake George to play such May games with you is troubling, my boy, very troubling, indeed," he pronounced from his vantage of sixteen years. He peered over at his brother and a knowing look flashed between them. "We may need to take this situation in hand."

"Do not trouble yourselves," Darcy quickly intervened. "A compass and a pound or so is not worth–"

"And how much will that leave you for next Term?" Richard shot back. "Not to mention what mischief he'll do next and ply you for more. It won't stop, Fitz, not until you let the little bugger pay the piper himself!"

D'Arcy nodded. "And the sooner the better! Allow Snake George to lead you on and you'll have more to answer for to Uncle Darcy than I'd care to owe."

"I've given my word." Darcy meant the sacred phrase to sound like a heartfelt principle but wondered if it did not instead sound more like a fainthearted excuse. The glances between the brothers were indecipherable, and for a moment there was an uncomfortable silence.

"A man's word is his word," Richard finally spoke.

D'Arcy nodded solemnly. "But there shall be no further 'word' given to snakes, here or at school. Agreed, Fitz?"

"Agreed!" Darcy pronounced with relief and thrust out his hand in the secret sign of their house at Eton. His cousins did the same.

"*Honorare et defendere!*" they all pledged and then fell back into their chairs, the tense moment assuaged and fellowship restored. Darcy grinned across the table at Richard, expecting an answering smile. Instead, he detected another furtive exchange.

"What is it, Richard? D'Arcy?" he demanded.

Richard's face flushed. "Fitz, D'Arcy overheard something. Our parents…" He stopped and looked at his brother, who nodded him on. "We could hardly credit it, but seeing Lady Anne today… Well, is it true that…that she's ill or…" He floundered, grew redder still, and then whispered, "worse?"

Darcy hesitate. The pain he had managed to put away for a few hours returned in a rush. The pretence that all was well was over. *They knew!* Yet, how could he say the words? Darcy looked helplessly at his cousins and then at his hands lying clenched in his lap.

"It is true, then." D'Arcy pronounced quietly.

Darcy looked up, his breath hitching in his chest. Both boys had turned pale, their eyes stark and disbelieving in spite of D'Arcy's assertion. "Yes," he answered, his voice strangled, "but you must not let on. She wants—" He couldn't finish, wasn't sure himself what she had meant.

"Dignity," D'Arcy finished for him. "And dignity she shall have. Never fear, Fitz, Christmas shall be merry, and I believe we've made a start."

"What?" Richard asked for them both.

"Your 'dodgy' snowball, Young Idiot!" his brother replied. Richard began to protest. "No, don't worry; I'd have done the same if I could look as innocent as you! But, Fitz," he addressed Darcy, "did you see Lady Anne? She thought it was marvellous! Every time she looked at my father tonight, she started to laugh. That's the ticket!"

"Make her laugh?"

"Make merry," D'Arcy corrected. "Just as we always do at Christmas—

"Just as they expect us to do, but more so!" Richard was warming to the task.

"Within reason and with some forethought," D'Arcy amended. "We don't want Father carrying through with his threat."

"Hmm, quite so!" Richard mused, "The possibilities..."

The brothers looked at Darcy.

~ ~ ~ ~ ~ ~ ~ & ~ ~ ~ ~ ~ ~ ~

"Within civilized limits!" Lord Matlock sternly enjoined his sons and his nephew the next morning but then cast an uneasy look at his brother-in-law. "Darcy, are you quite certain of this? The whole idea makes my blood run cold!"

Fitzwilliam and his cousins looked now to his father, their faces under strict regulation. "Supplicants all," D'Arcy had warned before they requested audience with their sires. "If we look too eager, we will be suspect. My father is a canny one," he had reminded his cousin. "He will not give leave if we appear overly anxious."

A genuinely amused smile spread across Darcy's face as he surveyed the boys' earnest countenances. "Matlock," he laughed, "you exaggerate abominably! What harm can there be? It sounds like something we did at their age."

"Take your life in your hands if my progeny's involved!" Matlock interrupted with a snort. "But if it will bring a smile to my sister's countenance, I'll not stand against it. Be it on your head, Darcy."

"Anne will adore it; I promise you."

Lord Matlock turned back to the boys with a sceptical eye. "Lord of Misrule, indeed!"

~ ~ ~ ~ ~ ~ ~ & ~ ~ ~ ~ ~ ~ ~

The cousins spent the rest of Saturday securing costumes for the evening's celebration of Misrule and skating on the frozen expanse of Pemberley's pond. Supper that evening was a patchwork of suppressed excitement, anxiety, and rigid good manners for Darcy as he and his cousins strove mightily to give no occasion for rescinding their plans. Richard fairly twitched with anticipation. He was firmly reminded of his duty by the occasional warning frown from his brother, who, at sixteen years of age, comported himself with a polish and ease among the adults that Darcy could only admire.

Although they were only family this year, the meal was conducted formally in the great dining hall, in accordance with Pemberley tradition. Lady Anne would brook no less.

The candelabras were lighted down the entire length of the table and the room was redolent with the scent of evergreens and spice. Bowls of clove-encrusted apples and oranges and mounds of nuts, both natural and sugar glazed teased Darcy's senses while the servants quietly served, then removed each course.

Almost did the tableau before him lull him into complacency. But a closer examination of his parents, aunt, and uncle disclosed a studied cheerfulness wholly unlike the repartee that was their usual custom. They, all of them, were making a gallant attempt to comply with Lady Anne's wishes that her illness be ignored and that Christmas be celebrated at Pemberley as it always had been. Yet, Darcy could see how the pretence they maintained wore on his mother, and it tore at his heart.

At last, they were dismissed to their preparations as the ladies retired to the Yellow salon and the men to Pemberley's gun room. Once out of his father's sight, Richard raced to the stairs with a whoop that brought his brother up behind him to deliver a warning cuff.

"Ouch!" Richard protested.

"Quiet, Idiot!" D'Arcy warned, then he turned to Darcy, who had not yet gained the stairs. "Coming?" With a slow nod, Darcy turned away from a last look at his mother as his aunt and Miss Barrows assisted her to the salon and ran to catch them up.

"The doors are closed; they're all inside!" Richard reported back from his post at the stairs. Earlier, they had raided the attic trunks for costumes, and Richard, as Lord Misrule, was tricked out in a coat from a much earlier time. Its hems almost swept the floor, but the unfashionably large brass buttons that adorned it and the voluminous pockets made it perfect for his part. An old-fashioned wig flowed almost to his waist to complete his costume, but his brother had not been satisfied.

"Where did you get those" Richard had looked suspiciously at the jars D'Arcy brought out.

"Something from school…never mind, just be still!" D'Arcy had commanded as he powdered his brother's face white and painted red rouge circles on his cheeks, mouth, and the tip of his nose and then had finished him off with a black patch at the corner of his mouth.

D'Arcy adjusted the pillows strapped under the green cloak that proclaimed him Father Christmas, as did the "beard" fashioned from the stuff of an old mattress. Darcy joined Richard in the hall. As befitted the character of Black Peter, Father Christmas's assistant, Darcy was dressed in a mis-match of old clothes pinned all over with colourful ribbons. His face was smudged black with cork and he sported an old red stocking, bedecked at the end with sleigh bells, as a cap.

"Are we ready?" Lord Misrule waved the thin, gilded chair leg that served as his sceptre.

"Yes, and you both look perfectly ridiculous!" laughed Father Christmas as they glided down the stairs.

A few candles in the drawing room were all the light they had allowed to the adults to make their way to the half-circle of chairs set up for them. The rest of the furniture had been moved aside and the rugs rolled up by the servants, leaving an area clear for the night's performance. As instructed, the servants had left crude stable lanterns and a chair for them in the hall. Darcy and D'Arcy took their lanterns and their stations on either side of His Lordship's "throne" and hoisted him to their shoulders.

"One, two, three," D'Arcy whispered, and the servants flung open the doors.

Now thrice welcome Christmas,
Which brings us good cheer,
Minced pies and plum-porridge,
Good Ale and strong beer;
With pig, goose and capon,
The best that may be,
So well doth the weather
And our stomachs agree!

A shout and laughter went up as, chanting and swinging their lanterns, they marched into the drawing room. "Oh, look at them!" Aunt Matlock laughed to Lady Anne, "Have you ever seen the like?"

"Oh, Good Lord! What have we agreed to, Darcy?" Lord Matlock groaned to his brother-in-law. "'Pon my word; it'll come to no good!"

"Marvellous!" Darcy called out, laughing and clapping his hands. "Marvellous!"

Encouraged, the boys continued circling the room.

Observe how the chimneys
Do smoke all about,
The cooks are providing
For dinner no doubt;
But those on whose tables
No victuals appear,
Oh may they keep Lent
All the rest of the year!

With holy and ivy
So green and so gay;
We deck up our houses
As fresh as the day,
With bays and rosemary
And laurel complete,
And everyone now
Is a king in conceit.

With that last line, Father Christmas and Black Peter set down His Lordship in the centre of the room, a lantern on either side of him. Lord Misrule bowed to the general applause but then motioned everyone quiet for the last verse.

But as for curmudgeons,
Who will not be free,
I wish they may die
On a three-legged tree.

Black Peter and Father Christmas solemnly bowed to Misrule and then helped him from his throne.

"But as for curmudgeons," His Lordship repeated in a now ominous tone, "who will *not* be free, I wish they may die on a three-legged tree! Father Christmas! You who can see into all men's hearts; be there any such here in *this* place tonight?"

"I regret it most keenly, My Lord, but it is so!" Father Christmas shook his head sorrowfully. "Black Peter, to your task!" At this command, Black Peter darted forward and executed a somersault that landed him precisely at the skirt hems of his mother and Aunt Matlock.

"Oh!" shrieked Lady Matlock in surprise as he rose before them. "What an excessively dirty Black Peter you are! Anne, what do you think? Have we behaved well enough this past year to pass the scrutiny of Father Christmas?"

Black Peter shook the bells at his cap's end at his aunt and then cocked his head at Lady Anne, awaiting her response. Her fingers lay upon her lips, but the laughter they suppressed was alive in her eyes.

"We shall certainly learn the answer shortly, Cecelia! Well, Black Peter, what is the verdict?"

Pulling out a small sack from his belt, Black Peter opened it with a flourish and peered inside. An expression of consternation washed over his face as he looked from Lady Anne to Lady Matlock.

"Oh, my dear," said Lady Matlock, "this does not bode well."

Black Peter shook his bells again at her and then reached into the sack. Suddenly, two oranges appeared in the air and, accompanied by their delighted squeals, fell neatly into the ladies' laps.

"Bravo!" called Mr. Darcy, clapping again. "Excellent, Black Peter!" With a curt bow in his direction, Black Peter skipped back to his companions.

"The ladies have pleased you, Father Christmas!" Misrule nodded approvingly. "But the ladies usually do. Now, sir, what of the men? It must be that this curmudgeon lies in their company."

"Black Peter, to your task!" commanded Father Christmas again. Black Peter shrank back and shook his bells violently. "To your task, sir!" Father Christmas cuffed his errant servant, who fell from the "blow" and rolled to the feet of his father and uncle to much laughter from the audience. Up he rose, blinking furiously and weaving from leg to leg as if concussed, then reached into his sack. "Oh!" cried the ladies as, again, an orange rose into the air.

"Well, well, Black Peter; bravely thrown!" Mr. Darcy displayed the orange on the tips of his fingers. "I believe that leaves only– "

"Hear, hear now!" Lord Matlock began to protest, but before he could finish, another object flashed into the air. "Coal! Now, really!" Black Peter skipped back to Father Christmas, shaking his bells vigorously.

"Matlock!" Misrule shook his sceptre at his father. "Give an account to Father Christmas of your plans for improvement! How shall you reform your ways in the year to come, sir?"

Lord Matlock rose from his chair. "My lord, you have mistaken me for someone else," he complained, "for I am *quite* virtuous, as these assembled here will attest. I am, sir, in no need of reform."

Shouts of laughter arose from the other adults. Lord Matlock settled back into his chair.

"A paragon, indeed," declared Misrule, "but, the laughter I hear declares your claim counterfeit! Come, sir, your plans for reformation are required of you!"

"Yes, your plans!" urged Mr. Darcy.

"Reforms, reforms!" cried the ladies.

Lord Matlock rose again and held up his hands for quiet. "In the face of betrayal on all sides–

Disapproving "Oh's!" and "Bad form, Matlock!" interrupted him.

"In the face of betrayal, I say, I will comply." He took a deep breath and in penitent tone announced, "I will hereafter refrain from wearing mismatched stockings."

An uproar ensued, the adults and the boys all calling down objections upon him. "Unacceptable! Unacceptable" bellowed Richard Misrule at his father.

"Untenable!" cried Lady Matlock. "Without his valet, Matlock cannot distinguish his pinks from his purples!"

"What! My own wife, my own family!" Lord Matlock, put a hand to his heart. "Oh, I am seriously misused!"

Everyone was laughing. Darcy's stomach ached from it. He looked at his family. His father was laughing, Richard was beside himself, his aunt was sunk back in her chair giggling. Most of all, his dear mother, with tears of laughter streaming down her face, had, for the moment, truly forgotten her troubles and pain. There was no pretence. There was no falsity. Rather, there was joy; joy in the companionship of family and love, great love, holding them all together.

Darcy stood there in his Black Peter regalia of tattered cloth and bell-tasselled cap and took in the noise and joyful chaos around him. This is how he would remember his mother: hands to her face as she looked about the room, her eyes twinkling and spilling over with mirth and goodwill. He felt the crushing sadness of the past week lift just a little. *This* is what Lady Anne had wanted and Darcy was satisfied.

Chapter 7

R emember, Fitz? It was about here that that fox popped up out of nowhere."

"I remember," Darcy reined in Trojan and looked about him trying to place a summer event from their childhood in the present winter's landscape. He and Richard had escaped the busyness of Pemberley on this Christmas Eve morning to ride out into the estate's surrounding wilderness. "And I remember your scoundrel of a dog would not give chase."

"Good old Cincinnatus!" Richard chuckled. "His fox chasing days were long over." He continued to chuckle, laughing harder until he was doubled over his horse's neck.

"What are you on about?" Darcy demanded, laughing at his cousin's laughter.

"Pater...last night! The old fox!" Richard gasped. "Stockings!"

"I am seriously misused!" Darcy quoted in stentorian tones and joined in Richard's glee. "He was marvellous! Did you see my mother?" Richard nodded. "I shall never forget it!"

They continued on only to pull up again when a herd of deer emerged from the wood ahead of them and flowed down to the banks of the Ere. Transfixed, the boys watched as the animals paused to drink from the river meandering through the snowy glen. Several of them cast wary eyes in their direction.

Darcy glanced over at his cousin. The previous evening had been a momentary relief, but the worries that beset him today were almost more than he could bear. The temptation to share at least some of them with Richard was so sharp that the words were out before he had quite thought them through.

"I'm in a mummer's play."

"What! You're in what?" Richard's eyes went wide.

"A mummer's play." Darcy hesitated while his cousin struggled to take in his meaning. "You've seen them: a performance with costumes and music and swordplay. Some of the village lads–

"Yes, yes, I'm well aware." Richard was overcome with surprise. "How…? When…?" Good heavens, does Uncle Darcy know?"

"No! Of course not!"

"I am astounded, Cousin!" A new respect shone from Richard's eyes. This was the kind of adventure he, himself, might engage in. He was responsible for many grey hairs on his father's head, but who would expect such a thing from his level-headed, well-behaved cousin, Fitzwilliam Darcy!

"Well, this is capital fun!" said Richard. "You must start from the beginning, Fitz, and tell all!"

Quickly, Darcy related how he had happened upon the group and become caught up in their endeavour and how he was now committed to performing with them. "I'm stuck in a hard spot and I need your help, Richard. The performance is this evening during the church service. Somehow, I must slip out without the family noticing."

Richard made a despairing noise at that, but Darcy continued. "Only for half an hour or so. The play is not long. I should be able to perform with them and return by the time the church service ends. It is just that there are some difficulties."

"Some!" Richard snorted. "I should say!"

"I must change into mummer dress. That is not so bad; but I need to bring my violin somehow."

Richard was ecstatic. This was exactly his kind of entertainment–daring, with just a hint of danger and disgrace. "So, you need to smuggle a costume and your violin and then devise an excuse for leaving the church service, perform, then get changed again, stow your violin, and get back as the service lets out. Gad, Fitz, this will be absolutely cracking if you can do it!"

"But, will you help me?"

"Of course!" Richard looked at him, much offended. "I would be quite disappointed if you had left me out of such a jolly adventure!" He paused and grew thoughtful. "Some lads in the village, you say. And a girl; you *did* mention a girl as well?"

Darcy nodded carefully, afraid of where his exuberant cousin would go with the information.

"Ahh, there's a sweetheart then!"

"Don't be stupid!" Darcy responded hotly.

"There's nothing wrong with having a sweetheart!" Richard waved away the insult. "Is she pretty? I should think she must be, or why would you–

"Bother with 'why!' I need your help with– "

"And you shall have it, Cousin; you and your sweetheart! What is her name?"

Darcy groaned. "She is *not* my sweetheart!"

"Are you sure?" Richard teased, but all his teasing could not prevent a small, sweet lightness to arise in Darcy's chest as he thought of Rosamund and the surprise she had for him that night.

~ ~ ~ ~ ~ ~ ~ & ~ ~ ~ ~ ~ ~ ~

Richard was better than his word. Between the two of them, they had contrived to stash Darcy's Black Peter costume—now his pedlar's gear—and his violin under the seats in the Darcy carriage just before it was rolled out of the carriage house for the horses to be hitched.

"Step one—done!" Richard announced with pure joy.

Racing back into the house, they exchanged their boots and coats for the splendid creations that were their Christmas clothes, brushed and re-tied their queues, and presented themselves in the hall for their hats and greatcoats with little notice from their parents or even D'Arcy.

Lady Anne had rested that afternoon and partaken of a light meal in her rooms. These had done her much good, for that evening she looked radiant. She also seemed more attuned to events around her.

"Fitzwilliam," she called him to her and, reaching out, tilted his face to her examination. "You look flushed, my dear. Are you feeling ill...or is it just that it is Christmas?"

Behind her, Richard froze at the question. His eyes flew to Darcy's.

"Christmas, Mama," Darcy replied uncomfortably. "Just Christmas."

"The carriages are here," his father called out. "Let's not keep the horses waiting!"

Outside, the air was brisk. The torch fires snapped and whistled against a night sky resplendent with stars. At the foot of the stairs, Samuel Coachman sat atop the Darcy carriage, a sprig of holly sewn onto his tricorne and the new muffler his wife had knitted him wrapped about his throat. Bells had been added to the horses' harness as well, and a continuous jingle emanated from both the Darcy and Matlock carriages as the horses stamped and shook themselves against the cold.

Wrapped carefully and protected from the slightest breeze, Lady Anne was led by her husband out to the steps and into the carriage where servants then hurried to surround her with hot bricks wrapt in flannel.

"Heigh-ho!" Richard whispered to him. "Step two—same carriage." With a broad wink, he hurried off to his family.

"Father, may I ride with Aunt and Uncle Darcy?"

"By all means, boy!" Lord Matlock replied. "But watch that you do not upset your aunt!"

"Father!"

"Go on with you. Don't keep Darcy's cattle waiting!"

"Yes, sir!" Richard came running back to the Darcy carriage. "May I ride with you, Uncle?"

"Climb in, but quickly," Mr. Darcy welcomed his nephew. Richard scrambled into the carriage and settled next to his cousin. "All right, then. Samuel," he called to the driver, "we're off!"

"Second step—done!" whispered Richard, as the driver whistled to the team and the carriage jerked to a start.

"Splendid!" Darcy whispered in turn.

Mr. Darcy observed them closely. "I might remind you two that Lord Misrule carried the day last evening, but decorum and respect are very much the order this evening."

"Be easy on them, dear," Lady Anne enjoined. "These boys have given me much pleasure. I'm sure I have not laughed so long or hard in an age as I did last night."

"Ah, yes. Well. I confess it did my heart good to see your brother brought to account so smartly. 'Twas well done, indeed!" Mr. Darcy chuckled softly.

The drive to Lambton required only half an hour in good weather. The snow and dark lengthened that by half, but, soon the glow from the church windows was visible from the outskirts of town. The closer they drew, the more people could be seen making their way to the square. Already, a small crowd was milling about and vendors were hawking their wares.

There! There they were! Darcy's stomach twisted into a knot of excitement and apprehension as the carriage skirted the square and came to a stop at the church door.

"Is that them?" Richard asked as they waited for Darcy's parents to descend.

"Yes, there's Jack and Teague," he pointed out his friends. "And...um...Rosamund. She's setting out the props."

"Ah, yes. A fine looking girl," Richard said appreciatively. He nudged Darcy and winked.

"Richard, please, it's not at all like that," Darcy whispered.

"Gentlemen?" Mr. Darcy called from the church steps where the rest of the family awaited them.

"Yes, sir," they both answered and, turning away from the square, followed their parents into the church.

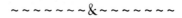

Some warmth from the heated bricks yet remained in the carriage as Darcy changed into his pedlar's garb and retrieved his violin. Throwing his greatcoat over all, he slipped out of the vehicle and around the church, running the last yards to the mummer's corner on the square.

> Here come I the Royal Duke of Blunderland,
> With my Broad Sword all in my hand,
> Where is the man that dares bid me stand...

Good! The performance has only just begun. He was in good time before he must make his own appearance. Looking about, he spied Rosamund in her Doctor clothes, awaiting her cue. The uneven torch light could not diminish the happy glow upon her face. It was her open, frank joy that drew him to her.

"Ah, Will!" Rosamund grabbed his arm and gave him a quick squeeze as, side by side, they watched the sword fight commence. "I knew ya'd come in time. Ain't it all just grand, then?"

"Grand!" Darcy affirmed, but when he turned his smile upon his companion, another's face loomed close behind and a foot above hers. The boy's pugnacious chin jutted below eyes that narrowed upon Darcy suspiciously. Darcy's brow rose in question.

"Um...Burle, this is Will. He's part of the troupe now."

"Humpf," was Burle's only acknowledgement before he turned his back on Darcy and looked back to the play.

"Burle is one of the Klympton mummers." Rosamund drew Darcy down to whisper. "He thinks I'm his girl, though I've done naught to make him say so. He's a bully, is Burle!"

Call the doctor, call old Quack
Take my donkey to bring him back.

"I'm on! Wish me luck!" Rosamund winked at him and skipped away to make her entrance. No sooner had she begun delivering her lines than Burle found his voice.

"Rosie's my girl, mate. So just you clear off."

"What do—" Darcy began.

"Clear off, I said!" Burle now turned to face him and flexed his fist before Darcy's nose. "Keep yer hands off'n her an' yer mind elsewhere, or you'll be that sorry. I promise ya. Rosie's taken, and there's the end of it." With his warning delivered, Burle sauntered off into the crowd.

Darcy stared after him in consternation. Had he just been challenged? Insulted? How did one deal with such surliness? Then, another more pressing concern arose. What was the time? Where was Richard?

Darcy whirled about and searched the crowd for his cousin and lookout. *Ah, there he was on the edge of the crowd, one eye on him and the other on the church door!*

"Safe, safe." Richard mouthed to him and waved him on. Darcy nodded and picked up his pedlar's sack in which lay his violin and ran over for his entrance.

> Here come I a Pedlar Chap,
> On my shoulder I car's my pack,
> I have ribbons for the Ladies fair,
> Ornaments to deck their hair,
> Patches for their pretty faces,
> High heeled boots and fine laces,
> Toys to please both great and small,
> And I've brought my Fiddle to please you all.

Darcy delivered his lines with a flourish, tossing out the various gifts of cheap ribbons and paper ornaments to their audience in the square as he spoke. Then, retrieving his violin from the sack he fiddled them a tune that sent not only the mummer's, but some in the crowd, also, to dancing and frolicking in the cold and joy of a clear Christmas Eve.

Darcy would have liked to continue, but suddenly Richard appeared near the front making frantic signs that could only mean that his time was up. Darcy dropped the violin from his chin and joined the troupe in their final speech.

A virgin unspotted the Prophets foretold.
Should bring forth a Savior which we do behold,
To be our redemption from Death, Hell and Sin,
Which Adam's transgressions involved us in.
So let us be merry, cast Sorrow away,
Christ Jesus our Savior was born on this day.

The applause and shouts of the crowd should not have affected him so, but the elation at having given satisfaction to so many almost made Darcy's heart burst. They had done it and done it well!

"Well done, Will!" Jack clapped him on the back. "Well done, indeed!"

"Hey, Will!" shouted Rob. "Did ya see that sword flight? The ladies were swoonin', they were!"

The troupe gathered into a knot as they all made the rounds, shaking hands with each other and well-wishers from the crowd. A tug on the ribbons at the back of his costume, brought Darcy around.

"Rosamund!" he smiled down into her dancing eyes.

"Your surprise, Will!" She tugged at the ribbons again and then pulled him around the corner of a vendor's stall.

"What is it, Rosamund?" he laughed, but in the next moment she threw her arms about his neck and was pressing a long, ardent kiss full upon his mouth! Surprise gave way to dizzy delight as he became more and more aware of her lips and her form pressed against him.

His arms began to lift of their own accord to embrace her when a hand clawed down the back of his neck, and he was jerked backwards by his collar far enough to recognize his assailant as Burle the Bully. Recognition was followed quickly by a numbing blow across his left temple that dropped Darcy to the ground.

"I tolds ya ta clear off!" Burle bellowed down at him. He turned away, but Darcy was already back on his feet. He grabbed at Burle to turn him back into his own blow, but both of them went down, twisting and punching, on the ground.

Darcy was only dimly aware of Rosamund's cry, "Lay off him now Burle Sikes, ya brute!" followed by numerous cries of "a fight, a fight!" Mummers and spectators of all descriptions rushed to form a noisy crowd that cheered and shouted encouragement to one or the other of the combatants.

"Hey, Burle, show 'em 'e can't mess wif a Klympton lad!" cried his fellow mummers.

Jack and Rob in turn shouted, "Take care of 'em, Will! Send 'em home bloody! He's no business comin' 'ere messin' with Rosie!"

All meaning was lost on Darcy. He could think of nothing except clutching, rolling, ducking, and punching. His head throbbed from the initial blow to his temple and soon his hands and knees were wet and raw from scraping the rocks and mud as he and Burle rolled about over the thin layer of snow. He could taste salty blood in his mouth. He landed some good punches as well, and he knew not all of the blood was his own; but Burle was taller and stronger and a born street fighter.

For the first time in his life, Darcy was possessed by an all-consuming instinct for survival. Neither boy could disengage. One would struggle to his feet only to be tackled and dragged again to the ground. Darcy's hands clutched and tore. His feet kicked. His lungs burned. His joints ached. His ears rang with grunts and curses and shouts from the crowd.

It was all Darcy could do keep his opponent off balance and prevent him from pinning him to the ground where he could use his fists most effectively. He heaved and twisted and turned to throw the larger boy off. Burle had the advantage for the moment, but Darcy managed to get his hand in Burle's hair and pull him down and to the side and they rolled about through the mud and snow yet again.

"Cease this instant!"

The expectation of compliance in his father's stern voice was followed by a sudden silence from the crowd. Darcy fell back from his assailant, gasping for breath, to look up into the red face of his father with Uncle Matlock beside him and a horrified Richard all looking down on him in the sudden stillness.

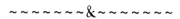

The ride home was a long journey dominated by the silent fury emanating from his father. His mother conversed in broken whispers while Darcy sat in humiliation, his head, nose, and hands bleeding and his mummers clothing covered with blood and mud and what Darcy suspected was some of Burle's blood as well. Richard had abandoned him and was riding back in the Matlock carriage. Darcy's single attempt to apologize was met with gruff contempt from his father.

"Not now, Fitzwilliam! Don't disgrace yourself further with excuses!"

When the horses were pulled up at Pemberley's door, his father motioned him to wait in the carriage. Mr. Darcy then turned to his wife and carefully ushered her within the hall and into the care of her maid. Peering out of the carriage, Darcy watched as his father looked after his mother while Miss Barrows assisted her to the stairs. He knew the moment when his father's thoughts turned back to him in the squaring of his shoulders and the stiffness of his father's manner on his return to the carriage.

"Fitzwilliam, you will proceed directly to your room and remain there for the rest of the evening. Reynolds will attend to your injuries, supervise your bath, and burn those clothes. You will see no one, speak to no one until you meet me in the stable tomorrow morning at seven o'clock sharp, whereupon we will discuss your future in this family. Do you understand me, Fitzwilliam?"

"Yes, sir...I am sorry, sir," he added, but his father only closed his eyes, shook his head, and walked into the house.

Chapter 8

Darcy spent a long and sleepless night. His wounds were not serious. Reynolds had cleaned several gashes on his head. A large goose egg had developed on his left temple where Burle Sikes had struck him initially. His hands were cut and scraped and a goodly part of his body ached. His nose felt swollen, but it had stopped bleeding early on. No, it was not his wounded body but the wound left by the loss of his father's regard that kept him awake.

He had rarely seen his father so enraged that he would or could not speak to him. His father's past discipline had always come quickly–short squalls that came and went, clearing the air with few lingering resentments. The number of trips to the stable for serious transgressions in his entire childhood could be counted on one hand. The protocol was always the same: a short discussion of his offence, a period for Darcy to explain himself and apologize, and, if the occasion required, a half dozen swift swats from a switch that hung in its assigned place near the stable gate.

Never had his father waited until the following day to administer his penalty. Never had Darcy spent so many hours under the dark cloud of his father's anger and disapproval. So Darcy was especially anxious as he awaited his father the next morning standing by the stable gate with the early Christmas morning sun slanting through the door.

He heard footsteps approach and looked up. His father looked tired, as if he hadn't slept any better than Darcy had. His anger from the night before was replaced by a deep weariness.

"Thank you for not keeping me waiting, Fitzwilliam. Let me look at you." His father inspected Darcy's head closely. "Reynolds said your injuries were superficial. That's fortunate. I trust you gave as well as you took."

"I believe I did, Father," Darcy said.

His father sighed deeply. "Do you understand why I am compelled to discipline you?"

"Yes, Father."

"I wonder if you do. What can you say to explain your behaviour last night, Fitzwilliam."

Darcy looked at his father briefly. The disappointment shown so clearly in his countenance that Darcy was forced to drop his eyes while he tried to collect his thoughts.

"I know I have acted rashly, Father. And I'm sorry for what happened. I did not consider the consequence of consorting with such a group...the mummers, I mean." Darcy looked up again. His father was listening intently.

"I had taken Trojan out for a ride to Lambton the day after our arrival from Town, but it was so windy and cold that I sought out some shelter. That's how I found them rehearsing in a barn. At first, I was merely curious to see what they were doing. I listened and watched them in secret. Their speeches were bad enough, but when I saw their sword-play, Father! Well, it was quite ridiculous, really!" Darcy looked up to see if his father shared his sense of the ridiculous. He did not.

"I couldn't stand to see it go forward. I spoke up. Jack and I fought with these silly wooden swords and I won." Darcy paused.

"Continue," his father said. His weariness seemed to deepen.

"Well, they wanted to learn what I could teach, Father. That's all. I showed them how to portray a convincing sword fight. One by one, I taught them all. And they accepted me. I met with them almost every day. Then they offered me a part and, blast it, Father, it was jolly good fun!"

His father blanched and hesitated as if at a loss for words to properly express his contempt.

"Jolly good fun, you say? Am I hearing you correctly? You would hold your family up to ridicule in a public place for some *jolly good fun?*" His father glowered at him.

"I know I've behaved badly, Father," Darcy added quickly. "I'm only trying to help you understand. After a time, my judgment was coloured by feelings of friendship. I came to feel an obligation to help...even in a public performance."

"In secret, Fitzwilliam! Without the knowledge of your parents! My only son, heir to my estate and my good name, sneaking out of a church service to masquerade in a street farce before drunks and rabble!"

Darcy could not respond. His actions so stated did indeed sound dreadful! They stood in a heavy silence, broken only by his father's laboured breathing.

"Your cousin, Richard, mentioned a girl. You were fighting over a girl?"

Ah, so Richard had been forced to confess his part in the affair.

"Rosie...ah, Rosamund. That was all a misunderstanding. You see, Burle, the boy who hit me, thought I was sweet on her. Rosie doesn't care a whit for him. But it all happened so quickly, I didn't have a chance to explain before we were rolling about on the ground and a crowd gathered and..." Darcy touched the bruise on his left temple.

"A fine state of affairs! And that's how I find you! Wallowing around in the dirt and filth like the lowest beggar's orphan!" His father paused to catch his breath. "And this girl, this..."

"Rosamund," Darcy supplied.

"This Rosamund. *Are* you sweet on her?"

"Well, no. I mean, I like her fine, Father, but, no, I'm not..." Darcy's blushing features said more in the affirmative than his words could possibly deny.

"Listen to me, Fitzwilliam Darcy," his father said. He held Darcy's shoulders and looked him in the eye. "If you're old enough to blush like that when a girl's name is mentioned, you listen to me. She's not for you! Do you hear me? She's not for you!"

The intensity of his father's voice froze Darcy.

"You are a Darcy. You are born to wealth and privilege. You must not abuse it, Fitzwilliam! I will tolerate a street mummer for a son a thousand times before I tolerate a cad. Such a girl can never be for you! A young man who would use his position of privilege to toy with a girl's affections is a scoundrel and worse than a scoundrel!"

"I...I haven't, Father." Darcy said uncertainly.

His father looked him deep in the eye for a long moment before nodding his head and stepping back.

"No, I don't believe you have, Fitzwilliam. I see no evidence of a corrupt heart here. You are young and this is a lesson for the future. But I do not want you to ever, *ever* neglect the duties and responsibilities attached to this family as you did last night. You are *different* than other young men. You are a Darcy. You cannot pursue pleasure at your whim. You cannot encourage every girl you fancy. Do you understand me, Fitzwilliam?"

"I think so, Father."

"Good. You 'think' so. I'm encouraged to hope then that this entire, unfortunate affair will have some positive consequences." Mr Darcy removed the switch from the wall of the stable and balanced it in his hand as he considered his son and heir.

"Fitzwilliam, if you would be so good as to bend over."

~ ~ ~ ~ ~ ~ ~ & ~ ~ ~ ~ ~ ~ ~

A soft knock at his door brought Darcy's head up from the pillow. The latch rotated, the door opened, and there was Richard, looking in at him anxiously. "May I come in, Fitz?" Darcy nodded, and his cousin slipped into his bed chamber, quickly closing the door behind him.

"Was it bad? Are you all right?"

"Last night or this morning?" Darcy cocked a brow at him and then winced at the pain.

"Oh! Well…both, but tell me about the fight!" Richard sat gingerly onto the bed next to Darcy, who lay there upon his stomach. "I missed some of it, you see, and I simply must have all the details."

"Missed it!" Darcy choked. "You deserted me?"

"Deserted?" Richard repeated, horrified. "No, no, Fitz! When I saw you and that fellow go down and the crowd gather around you shouting and yelling, I ran to find our parents. Father and Uncle were already wondering what had happened to us, and they could offer you more help than I."

When Darcy did not reply, he took another tack. "Can you forgive me, Fitz? I was worried about you; I couldn't think of anything else. That Sikes fellow, you know, looked awfully big and devilishly mean!"

The look of penitence on Richard's face was wonderfully pathetic, and Darcy would have laughed if his ribs were not protesting the very idea. "Richard, you corker! Stop looking at me like that!" he cried. His cousin's contrition turned into a grin. "Pax! You are forgiven!"

"So, *tell* me!" Richard returned to the point. "Did you give as good as you got?"

"I think so," Darcy replied slowly. "If the scrapes on my fists are any indication, I don't think his face looks any better than mine! Maybe worse!"

"Let me look at you," Richard demanded.

Humouring him, Darcy carefully stood up and held out his hands for inspection. Then he rolled up his sleeves and finally pulled up his shirt to display the bruises on his ribs. "My knees are scraped as well, but it is this lump on my skull and the nose that look the worst."

Richard assessed the wounds from several angles. "Oh, the nose is lovely! Shows you are no shirker. I don't know if you got a look at Sikes, Cousin, but I think he was thankful for your father's intervention. He lay there in the mud looking wonderfully beaten up and miserable long after you limped away. What a story to tell the fellows back at Eton! I am entirely envious!"

Darcy snorted. "I rather think not!" He touched his nose tenderly and carefully lay down on his side.

Richard sat back on the bed and shook his head. "Rather a bloody nose than what I endured on the ride home! Pater grilled me unmercifully and kept at me until I confessed everything, Fitz. If you'd heard him, you wouldn't blame me. The threats were horrendous!" Richard shuddered. "Loss of privileges and spending money were the least menacing! There were hints of physical discipline as well that made my blood run cold."

"Hmm." Darcy heard him with not the least bit of sympathy. "Any wounds suffered on my behalf to show?"

Richard had the grace to colour slightly. "Ahh...no. Pater's bite is unequal to his bark." Momentary embarrassment, however, was no deterrent. "How was it with *your* father? I was under the strictest of orders not to try to see you last night or until after breakfast this morning."

"Terrible," Darcy replied.

"Terrible...how?" his cousin prodded.

"Well, I doubt I shall be able to sit for Christmas dinner, for one," Darcy sighed. "But the weight of my father's utter displeasure was such that I hope never to know again."

"But, surely, he was pleased with how well you displayed to advantage in the fight!" Richard protested. "Good old Fitz—upholding the family honour!"

Darcy grimaced. "Besmirching the family honour, more like," he replied heavily, "and that is something I vow never do again."

~ ~ ~ ~ ~ ~ ~ & ~ ~ ~ ~ ~ ~ ~

Darcy knocked lightly on his father's library door and opened it slowly. "You sent for me, Father?"

"Ah, Fitzwilliam, come in." His father waved him to a chair in front of his desk.

"If it's all the same, Father, I will stand."

"I see. Of course." Comprehension spread across his face. "I've been talking with Mr. Wickham. I believe he has something that belongs to you."

Darcy nodded to Pemberley's steward, George's father. He was a short, sturdy man who had earned his father's trust over many years. It was a mystery to Darcy how this honest, straightforward man could possibly have sired the wily, calculating son who carried his name.

"Yes, Master Darcy. This was presented at the gatehouse early this afternoon by a young person from the village. She

113

said it belonged to you." Wickham held forth Darcy's violin and bow. He'd forgotten all about it during the chaos of the fight.

Darcy took the proffered items and said, "Thank you Mr. Wickham. I am glad to have this back."

"Well, then. I believe my business is done. I trust you will all have a most happy Christmas. I'll return and prepare for my own dinner." Wickham bowed. "Mr. Darcy. Master Darcy."

"Thank you, George. Give our blessings to Ellie and young George," Mr. Darcy said as Wickham took his leave. He turned his attention to his son.

"Well, I trust this is the last reminder of last night's unpleasantness, Fitzwilliam. I wish to declare this episode behind us. I want no unhappy feelings between us."

Mr. Darcy approached his son, hugged him firmly, and stood back. "You have survived a most terrible lapse of judgment with my love and respect for you intact. I trust that you have learned a lesson, Fitzwilliam; a lesson in what a gentleman owes to those below him in station and what he owes to his family's prestige and honour. Are we of one mind on this?"

"Yes, Father. Let my future behaviour speak for itself. We are of one mind."

The family gathered in the drawing room in anticipation of Reynolds's announcement that Christmas dinner was served. The events of the previous evening and Darcy's careful movements were not remarked upon. To the contrary, memory of the events seemed to have fled wholesale, a consensus which Darcy was only too happy to uphold. Sundry, small gifts had been exchanged earlier, and the present conversation tended toward their admiration or the evening when Lord Misrule and company had so entertained them.

Restricted by his various pains, Darcy took up a position near the hearth and leaned against the mantle. To his surprise, he discovered it to be the perfect vantage from which to observe his beloved family in all their candour. D'Arcy and Richard were at a table where they played at a game of cards which seemed to provoke as much discord between them as pleasure. Aunt and Uncle Matlock teased each other good naturedly over her propensity to knot up her bonnet strings and his spoiling of a hunting dog which she declared him to love more than her.

Darcy's father sat on a cushion at his wife's feet, her hand in his as he focused all his attention on the quiet words she addressed to him and her brother and sister-in-law. Observing them, Darcy's heart filled. How he loved them, loved them all! And, save for a miracle, this would be the last Christmas they would be together.

A tear formed at the corner his eye. Darcy hastily dashed it away. *No good to be a baby about it!* He straightened from his stance just as the door opened. *Reynolds?* Everyone looked up, but it was Nurse with a bright-eyed Georgiana on her hip.

"Mama!" she cried and reached out to her mother before Nurse could even curtsy. Darcy strode to her as quickly as he could and held out his arms.

"Here, Dolly; I'll take you to Mama."

Georgiana nodded vigorously and began to wiggle away from Nurse. "Fis take!" she pronounced over and over until Nurse relinquished her into his grasp.

"I wanted Georgiana with us today," Lady Anne explained while Darcy brought her to their mother and set her gently in Lady Anne's lap. "I wished for *all* of us to be together this Christmas day!"

At that moment, the door opened again and a well-pleased Reynolds announced that everything was in readiness.

~ ~ ~ ~ ~ ~ ~ & ~ ~ ~ ~ ~ ~ ~

Walking in formally behind his parents and his aunt and uncle, Darcy heard their gasps of pleasure before spying their cause. The entire dining room was a cornucopia of delights to the eye as well as the palette. Gay ribbons of silver, gold, and red had been added to the greenery that festooned the walls, sideboards, and table. The best silver had been laid beside china so delicate that Lord Matlock declared that he feared to breathe in its presence lest the mere act crack them asunder.

Dish upon dish lay in splendour upon the table and the sideboards, some covered with silver lids and others open to scent the air with wonderful effect.

Georgiana, who was again in Darcy's arms, crowed with delight at the decorations and tugged at his neck cloth to call his attention to all the wonders. "Look, Fis, look!" she commanded.

"I see them, Sweetling," he laughed and settled her in the high chair especially brought down from her nursery.

"I'll see to her, Master Darcy," one of the servant girls assured him with a curtsy. He nodded to her and went to stand next to his uncle.

"Please, be seated, everyone." Mr. Darcy motioned to the servants to pull back the chairs. When they were settled, Reynolds advanced to his master's side and removed the lid from the first course, a fresh pea soup garnered from the trays of plants cultivated in the estate's greenhouse. A ladle was placed close to hand. "Thank you, Reynolds." Mr. Darcy turned to his guests. "Shall we begin?"

Remove after remove was presented on shining silver platters. Roast goose with bread sauce, Brussels sprouts with chestnuts, cranberry sauce, and roast potatoes, a haunch of venison, and smoked salmon. The second course featured a roast of beef, pheasant, and rabbit. These were garnished with jellies and crèmes, fruit tarts, assorted vegetables, iced punch and a variety of wines. Toasts were offered to family and to friendship and, finally, to the flaming plum pudding that Cook proudly brought to the table.

It was a Christmas "bang-up to the mark," as Richard would later tell his classmates at Eton, spoiled only by the fact that his cousin Darcy had been obliged to stand through it all.

~ ~ ~ ~ ~ ~ ~ & ~ ~ ~ ~ ~ ~ ~

Darcy stepped quietly around Miss Barrows and into his mother's chambers. His mother's maid had knocked softly at his door with a summons from Lady Anne that she wished him to attend her before she retired for the evening. Only a few candles lit her sitting room and the bedchamber beyond. One flickered at her side as, swathed in shawls, she reclined on the divan. The light was faint, but Darcy could see plainly that although the holiday had exhausted her, she was content.

"Fitzwilliam!" She held out her hand to him. Darcy advanced into the room and took hold of it as Barrows furnished him with a stool and pillow to sit by his mother's side.

"Mama," he murmured, "you are tired."

"Yes, dear one; but not so tired that I can sleep without first knowing for certain that all is well with you, my son."

117

Her other hand rested lightly on his jaw and tipped him this way and that as she inspected his wounds with a worried eye.

"Truly, it is not so bad, Mama."

"Hmm," she responded, unconvinced. "And what of the rest of you?"

"Nothing over which you should worry, I promise!" he assured her even as he winced from a soft probe of her finger. That she should spend a moment of concern over his folly mortified him!

"Rather, I must beg your forgiveness for my behaviour last night. It should have been my object to bring you comfort." He bent and kissed the hand that still held his. "But, I fear that I have been foolish and brought trouble and disgrace, instead."

"Indeed? Can this be so?" Lady Anne regarded him closely, but her lips betrayed her and curved into a compassionate smile.

"It has been greatly impressed upon me by my father that it is so!" He grinned back at her, but it faded as he continued. "And I must agree with him. I did not think...I did not know..." He shook his head. "But, I understand now, and it shall be my earnest study that the name of Darcy is never again in danger of reproach."

"Of that, I have no doubt," his mother whispered as she contemplated his features. "Oh, you look so much like your father in this solemn attitude! I almost see what you will be when you are a man grown—so grave and reserved!" She ran her fingers through his hair and brought them to rest on the side of his face. "Never forget this Christmas, Fitzwilliam, for it has been the finest I could ever have wished for."

~ ~ ~ ~ ~ ~ ~ & ~ ~ ~ ~ ~ ~ ~

When Darcy took up his violin to tune it later that evening, he heard a dry rattle come from within. A shake confirmed that there was something skittering back and forth inside. He turned the instrument over and shook it several times before a neatly folded square of paper fell out onto the floor. Picking it up, he carefully unfolded it and read:

> I know your name is not Will. How surprised we
> all was to find you a Darcy. No matter. I would
> kiss you all over again.
> Rosamund

Darcy smiled as he read the untutored script of her handwriting. *Rosamund!* He thought of her eyes, with their sparkle and wit, and that thrilling intimacy he felt when she pulled his arm and whispered in his ear. He would not forget her kiss, that was certain...or all that followed!

She is not for you!

Note in hand, he drifted over to the window that looked out upon the frozen, snow-encircled pond and leaned against the pane. A number of Pemberley's servants were still about, torches in hand or wedged in the snow, as they prepared the pond area for the morrow's Boxing Day festivities. Soon after breakfast, he would accompany his father to the servants' hall and, in his mother's stead, assist him in presenting them their Christmas gifts and free them to enjoy the rest of the day in games, competitions and, finally, a country dance, all at Pemberley's expense. It was what the Darcys did; what they had done from generations past.

This was his heritage as heir of the Darcy name and estate—Pemberley. *Pemberley.* His heart swelled as he watched a handful of men clear away the new snow for skating and sledding on the frozen pond. Their shouts and laughter sounded faintly through the heavy window. He felt a sudden rush of emotion for his home—the lands, the buildings, the fields and streams, the woods, and the countless servants, caretakers, and tenants who depended upon his family for their own happiness.

He thought of his brave mother. Soon, there would be only he and his father and little Georgiana to carry on this legacy. And some day, in the future, the responsibility for Pemberley would rest with him alone. Well, not exactly *alone*, for he would have a wife and children and an heir in turn.

The weight of all that had happened and all that he was called to be settled firmly upon Darcy's shoulders. He straightened and looked down at the note in his hand. *Rosamund.* She had kissed him only a day ago, yet he felt different, understood more about himself. In some strange way, the events of the week seemed to have happened to someone else—a child who was now a distant memory. *Can one change so quickly?* he wondered.

Crossing the room, he crouched before the hearth and carefully, gently fed the note to the flames.

—&—
End
—&—

CPSIA information can be obtained at www.ICGtesting.com
Printed in the USA
LVOW081511250212

270412LV00001B/170/P